w x2

The Last Mann

Jubal Mann was the closest he'd ever come to realising a long-held dream. With all his experience following the wild and dangerous cattle trails, from the Rio to Canada, he figured he could start a new breed of cattle: Longhorn Cross with imported Red Angus.

Mann was convinced that the best of the hardy, self-sufficient Longhorn combined with the meat-bearing quality of the Angus would put top-notch steaks on the plates of a nation, and dollars in his pocket.

However his past came back to haunt him: just as he had his dream within reach, killers moved in and he found himself with his back to the wall, and a smoking gun in each hand.

The Last Mann

Hank J. Kirby

A Black Horse Western

ROBERT HALE · LONDON

© Hank J. Kirby 2011
First published in Great Britain 2011

ISBN 978-0-7090-9215-5

Robert Hale Limited
Clerkenwell House
Clerkenwell Green
London EC1R 0HT

www.halebooks.com

Typeset by
Derek Doyle & Associates, Shaw Heath
Printed and bound in Great Britain by
CPI Antony Rowe, Chippenham and Eastbourne

PROLOGUE

GRAVEYARD COUNTRY

They first saw him riding out of the sunset, an indistinct blob against the quivering air of the burning sky, far out on that part of the Texas plain known as Graveyard Country.

It was Macy who saw him first and he called Ma. Such was the urgency in his eleven-year-old voice, that Liza Mann paused at her floured board where she was preparing flapjacks, quickly wiped off her forearms and reached down for the old Spencer carbine hanging from the wooden pegs driven into the thick earthen wall of the sod house: well, mostly soddy – the front was adobe, but only the front.

She hurried out on to the gallery – most folk were beginning to call such extensions to the house 'porches' at this time. The well-used carbine was cocked and ready.

The tousle-haired boy, Macy, had climbed on to the rail now and was pointing into the ruddy glow. 'I seen him, Ma – a rider. He has to be headin' this way, don't he, Ma?'

'No place else for him to go,' agreed the woman, weather-bitten, forties, mostly-grey hair pulled back into a bun-knot held in place by an old tortoiseshell comb. She had been a handsome woman, once, still retained some of her looks beneath the sun-damaged, work-worn skin and in the bright blue eyes that squinted now.

Frannie, the eldest daughter, just twelve, her body not yet starting to blossom enough to show a change in contours beneath her faded, patched, but clean dress, handed her mother the old brass field glasses Pa had brought back from his Cavalry days.

Ma passed Macy the Spencer: he had been shooting and bringing in game for the table for the last four years. His small dirty thumb hooked the hammer sear, ready to cock again if necessary.

'Lone man,' Ma said, adjusting focus. 'Looks weary, way he's slumping in the saddle.' *But his head was active enough as he looked around: a cautious rider, which was wise, with renegade Comanche bucks from the Agency making devilment among the settlers now and again.*

'What'll we do, Ma?' asked Frannie anxiously, pushing strands of light-coloured hair back from her freckled face.

Liza Mann swapped the glasses for the carbine.

6

'We welcome him: that's the way it should be. If not. . . .' She slapped a hand lightly against the Spencer. 'Macy, go fetch the others. Bring 'em in from wherever they are.'

'Aw, Ma, I wannna see who it is. . . .'

Ma gave him a sidelong look, one of the 'obey-me-now' looks she had, and Macy sighed, handed the field glasses to Frannie who poked out her tongue as he vaulted the rail and ran around the side of the house, calling to his brothers and sister. Will and Saul were younger than him, and then there were the twins; Andy – in bib-and-brace overalls that Macy had once worn himself, then, when he outgrew them, passed on down to other siblings as they arrived – and Hal, the other twin, in a dirt-smeared shirt and short trousers. There should've been another, older brother, but he had gone off to war.

It wasn't a particularly large family for the times, and Ma only noticed it when it came to feeding time, and the larder was lean . . . or wash-day! *She wished Melvin, her husband, was here. But, times being lean, he had taken work as a wagonmaster for an emigrant group making their laborious way to Utah. . . . She didn't know when – or if – he would be back, though she swiftly pushed that small, big-meaning word from her mind. . . .*

The rider arrived just as it was time to light the lamps. He was a large man, thirties, she judged, a mite younger than Mel. He wore a faded army jacket with frayed captain's bars. He had a face built for worry – or was it held-in anger? – and he got right down to business.

'Miz Mann? Ah, someone gave me the right directions then.' He had a deep voice, a mite harsh, likely because of the long, dry ride. 'Name's Stone, Gabriel Stone. Most folk just call me Gabe or sometimes Cap'n, occasionally Skipper from my riverboat days.' He slapped his jacket and dust puffed from the faded cloth.

He asked permission to water his horse, and himself, at the well and Ma sent Macy scurrying to bring a pail of water. After he had had a dipperful, and had held the pail for the dusty, weary mount, he spoke over his shoulder, unfazed by the gallery now packed with the staring Mann family.

'I'm powerful sorry to arrive this time of night, right on your supper time I suspect. . . .'

She wasn't sure if it was a hint or not, but she had certainly been going to invite him to eat with them.

'You're welcome to share our vittles, Captain.'

He looked mildly annoyed, shook his head and his long black hair lifted dust from the shoulders of his jacket.

'Ma'am, I wasn't hintin' to be asked.'

'You don't have to, nor does anyone visiting the Manns.'

'I thank you kindly, ma'am, but I have to be on my way. Got to be in Salt Fork by tomorrow mornin'.'

'Why – you'll need to ride all night!'

'Won't be the first time, nor the hundredth, ma'am.'

'The night is dangerous out here, Captain – Renegade bucks from the Agency on the mesa. . . .'

He smiled, showing large yellow teeth. 'I've had my share of Indians, too, Miz Mann.'

She felt herself flush slightly as she nodded. Of course! He was an ex-army man. She ought to've thought before she spoke.

'I-I stopped by to bring you some – some bad news, I'm afraid . . . quite – well, very bad. . . .'

Liza Mann felt the twist in her insides. Her hands clutched the Spencer so tightly the knuckles seemed as if they would pop through the taut skin. She had had a premonition – for weeks now! A feeling that all was not well with Mel. She had irritably thrust it aside but it came back heavily to her in the long dark hours spent in the lonely bed.

Now, Dear God, let him be safe!

'My – husband?' she asked tentatively and heard the indrawn breath of the gawking kids. Little Andy with the golden curls began to sniffle, ran in close to Ma and clutched at the woman's skirts, sensing unwelcome news.

'Oh, Ma! Not Daddy! Nothing's happened to my Daddy, has it?'

'Hush, child.' Ma forced herself to speak calmly, patting the golden curls, feeling the thin little arms clutching at her through the calico. 'The Captain hasn't said anything about harm coming to our father.'

'But – but he *looks* like he's going to!'

Stone smiled thinly. 'That child is perceptive, ma'am. Unusual in a boy child, specially so young. Fact, with those curls he could easily pass for a

9

gal. . . . Ooops! I'd better not say that, I guess! My apologies, young feller.'

'Never mind Andy, Captain,' Ma said kind of tersely, the strain welling up in her. 'What news have you?'

He seemed uncomfortable, gestured briefly. 'The children. . . ?'

'It'll affect us all eventually, Captain, so they might as well hear it now. Please!'

He dropped his gaze to Andy. 'I'm afraid his intuition is right, ma'am. It's about your husband and . . . it's not good.'

The children gathered around her and some started to wail until she had to harden her voice and call for quiet. Captain Stone looked mighty uncomfortable.

'It's the worst kinda news, ma'am. There was an Indian attack on the wagon train he was leading through the San Juan Mountains in Colorado. The entire train was wiped out: men, women, children. . . . A massacre. Not a single survivor.'

It was dreadful on that ruddy-lighted gallery with the crying children; Liza Mann fighting to hold in her own tears, wanting to wail and scream uninhibitedly like her brood: she knew she couldn't hold back much longer.

Captain Gabe Stone was obviously distressed at having to deliver such news and swung aboard his horse, wanting out of there as quickly as possible.

'My deepest sympathy, ma'am. I-I've done my duty and must be on my way.'

'Wait! How – how can you be sure?'

He heaved a sigh, murmured, 'I was the scout – away when it happened. I came back to such. . . . Well, I'm sure, Miz Mann, an' I'm awful sorry. I wish you all luck.'

She couldn't speak, watched through welling tears as he wheeled his horse and rode out into the darkening land.

Graveyard Country. Strangely numbed now as she herded the family inside the sod-section of the adobe-fronted house. She thought it would claim them all eventually; two stillborn children rested in its dry earth on the rise behind the house already. Mel had even marked out, with lines of rocks, the plot he fancied for himself and Liza when their time came, to rest side by side, for Eternity.

Now there wouldn't even be the comfort of him nearby, a last resting place she could visit and – weep. . . .

She could hold back no longer. Her shoulders began to shake and the long, hard sobs wracked her work-worn body. Suddenly, it was the children comforting her instead of the other way round.

It was black as the inside of a gunbarrel when Captain Stone reached the rise, slightly to the north of the lonely trail he had taken out to the Manns' place.

There were straggly trees and brush here, but another rise behind prevented them being silhouetted against the sky that was beginning to prick with stars, like someone lighting a million lanterns, one by one.

Stone showed no great surprise when a man in a crumpled hat stepped out of the shadow, a cigarette dangling from a corner of his mouth. 'That the right place, Cap'n?'

Stone dismounted and slapped the cigarette out of the man's mouth, causing him to suck in a sharp breath as he stepped back quickly, dropping a hand to the butt of the six-gun holstered on his right hip.

'Don't be stupid, Gale – I told you no smoking before I left. And I sure don't want a gunshot to give us away when I kill you – which I will do if you don't take your hand away from that Colt. If I jam the muzzle tight into your belly before I fire, that ought to muffle it.'

Gale swallowed and lifted his hand quickly from his gun butt. Someone behind him in the shadows snorted quietly. Captain Stone flicked his dark gaze that way.

'Same applies to you all. Yeah, it's the Mann place, all right, and I left 'em in tears, weepin' for poor old Mel, the lousy son of a bitch!' He had to pause as his throat started to close with emotion. He dragged down a steadying breath. 'Get Leaping Dog up here.'

The brush rustled and a tall painted Comanche stepped out, cradling a short-barrelled rifle with a wired-up stock. Stone smelled the grease on his gleaming body, the foul breath from eating raw horsemeat and guzzling whiskey that tasted like acid. The Indian said nothing.

'The front of the place is adobe,' Stone told him quietly. 'Looks thick, but the windows, even with the shutters and loopholes, are the most vulnerable. They are the easiest, can be smashed open. You savvy?'

Leaping Dog nodded once, jerkily. 'Savvy.'

'The walls of the house are sod, three foot thick, I'd guess. The roof has buffalo grass growing on it, two feet high – dead and dry. It'll burn, but there could be a couple of feet of sod underneath it. I couldn't see properly, it bein' so dark inside the house, and the door only partly open. . . . But it shouldn't be a problem for you. Savvy? No problem. Destroy the house and kill them all.'

'Savvy.'

'Go get it done, then!'

'More better you give us Henry guns now. Make sure we kill 'em all.'

'Ah, no, you don't. I promised you a case of Henry repeaters after you massacre the Manns. You bring me the scalps . . . *all* scalps. OK? Then you get the guns.'

The Indian grunted, cold eyes gazing deep into Stone's rugged face. 'No Henrys – you got no more life.'

'Yeah, yeah, I know. You'll get your guns tonight, but you'll have to wait and ride a few miles to where the ammunition is stashed tomorrow.'

'You not trust Comanche.'

'Damn right there!'

*

13

There were ten in Leaping Dog's band, their inbred hatred of the whites fuelled by raw whiskey, which, in turn, boosted their blood lust. Gabe Stone and his three white companions sat their mounts on the crest of the rise – it didn't matter if they were silhouetted now – and watched the Indians sneak in towards the distant house where no lights showed.

Stone smiled slowly: that woman was playing it safe. Well, they'd told him the Manns had been scratching out a living here for almost ten years. Damn fools thinking they could make their fortune in this kind of country, though he had heard that ten years ago the Graveyard Country was lush with belly-deep grass which had all disappeared, never to grow again for some reason, after the big drought of '58.

'Well, they mightn't've made a *livin'* here, but they sure as hell are gonna make a *dyin'!*' he said quietly, chuckling.

Even this far off, the din was terrible: gut wrenching blood-curdling war cries, rifle shots. He could hear that old Spencer banging away from the house, and smiled again: that woman! Protecting her brood against all odds!

But not for long.

Soon the roof was blazing, a funeral pyre reaching high into the Texas night sky under a thick column of rising sparks that obliterated the stars. The war cries had been replaced with inhuman screams of varying degree: *Stone reckoned he could differentiate between the woman's and the childrens' screams as Leaping Dog and his butchers went about their bloody work.*

It was music to his ears: *he only wished Mel Mann had*

lived long enough to witness this, the fulfilment of Gabe Stone's vow to destroy the entire Mann family, wipe them out.

It was all over in an hour-and-a-half.

Then the Indians came back, spattered with blood and bits of gore, drunk on blood-lust as if they had downed a gallon of rotgut moonshine. But if they were looking for praise from Gabe Stone they were mightily disappointed.

Leaping Dog dropped a sodden flour sack at Stone's feet. The white man upended it, holding it by one corner so as not to get blood on his fingers, and tipped out the gory trophies. He poked at the mess, separating the scalps with a twig, counting them—

'Gimme some light!' he snapped, a harshness in his voice making the white men jump, the Indians tense. Gale hurriedly snapped a vesta into flame on a horny thumbnail and held it close, the flame reflecting in the wet flesh of the scalps.

Stone roared and surged to his feet, his face wild and close to being demented as he turned on Leaping Dog, whipping out his Colt and ramming the muzzle up under the startled Comanche's jaw. He could hardly speak for passion.

'Where's the blond scalp – from that kid, Andy? Where *is* it, you miserable piece of dung!'

Leaping Dog made guttural sounds and lifted his bloody knife from his belt. Stone dropped the gun hammer and stepped back quickly from the falling Indian as the rest of the raiders froze where they stood in the brush.

15

Gale jumped. 'We still gonna give 'em the Henrys?'
'Sure! One bullet at a time!'

CHAPTER 1

CHEYENNE

It was raining in Cheyenne. *Rain – rain – rain.*

Not just a heavy shower, but a downpour that mired the streets, turning them into mud slides and semi-bogs; chocolate-coloured streams overflowing deep gutters dug beside the boardwalks, making the walks themselves dangerous, sliding, skidding places for the unwary.

Roofs spurted like firehoses, others spilled over sagging gutters in drenching waterfalls. It was no time to be out of doors, for man or beast.

The tall man just about to leave the protection of the livery paused in the double doorway to adjust his poncho, pulling it so he could grip a big tear between finger and thumb from underneath, pinching it tight enough to keep the top part of his clothing dry. His trousers were already soaked and mud-spattered from racing his horse through the

17

increasing downpour, trying to reach shelter before it turned into a cloudburst.

He was a little late but hoped to get no wetter than he already was. He had left his warbag with the horse in the stall, and given the hostler a silver dollar to take good care of his mount and his belongings.

In the doorway now, gathering himself for a dash across the mire of the street, he jumped hurriedly aside as a rider ran his horse through the double doorway and hauled rein violently, skidding right alongside him, spraying mud.

'Sorry, friend,' the rider said without really sounding sorry, rain running from his beard. 'Kinda muddy.'

The tall man made a 'damn-it-all' hand gesture and, as he was about to move, he heard the hostler call: 'What name was that, sir?'

Sir! That dollar must've have been well spent! He raised his voice above the roar of rain:

'Jubal Mann.'

'Thanks, Mr Mann. I'll take care of your things.'

Mann dashed out into the rain, his figure becoming blurred within the first half-dozen steps.

The bearded man dismounted slowly, a wet bulk in his patched slicker, pushed back his sodden hatbrim and squinted. But he couldn't see the man who had just left, now swallowed up by the rain. He led his mount towards the rear where the hostler was rubbing down a mud-spattered roan. He glanced up, saw the new arrival and said casually, still working on the roan, 'Take any vacant stall, friend. Oh, Mr

Sievers, ain't it?'

The big man nodded. 'This one next door'll do. Say, that feller just left, you know where he's stayin'?'

The hostler, abundant dark and lank hair awry, shook his head and the man in the aisle thought he was telling him he didn't know where the other was staying. But it was only to get the long strands out of his eyes.

'Said he was bookin' in at the Regal. 'Cross the street, if you can make it without drownin'.'

The bearded rider backed his grey mount into the stall and began to off-saddle. 'I know where it is.'

The rain had eased some – a little! – by the time Mann walked into the foyer of the Regal, a frame, two-storeyed building with worn carpets adding to the hazard of a rickety stairway leading to the floor above. He had registered and gone up to his room by the time the bearded man entered and tilted back his hat, cursing as some of the collected water in the curl brim trickled down his back.

'If you're after a room, sir,' spoke up the bored and balding clerk behind the counter,' I'm afraid we've just booked the last one. The bad weather, you know.'

The bearded man flicked him a glance from bleak eyes that made the clerk step back half a pace, blinking once at the unwarranted hostility there. He was so surprised that he didn't protest as the man spun the register and looked at the last entry, his wet fingers smudging some of the writing.

'Careful there!' said the clerk automatically but backed up another half pace as the cold eyes lifted to his face again and rested there briefly. The bearded man read the scrawled signature.

Jubal Mann – Creede, Colorado.

'Feller's come a far piece,' he murmured, the voice low enough to make the clerk hesitate and then decide the man was talking to himself.

'Maybe I could share a room with this feller Mann. . . ?' suggested Sievers.

The clerk was pleased to reply, 'Afraid Room 27 is a single, mister. You may find a place at one of the rooming houses. . . .'

He leaned over the counter to point the direction but the bearded man was already walking across the lobby and out into the rain.

The storm eased within the hour and Jubal Mann was pleasantly surprised when he opened the door to a knock and found the hostler standing there, with his warbag and his rifle wrapped in a piece of burlap.

'Thought maybe you were needin' fresh clothes, Mr Mann.'

'Well, you're a mind-reader – and you've earned yourself another dollar.'

The hostler took the coin, started to go, but turned back. 'Er – mebbe none of my business, but that feller almost rode you down in the doorway? Name's Sievers. Comes into town occasionally from I dunno where. He was askin' after you. I – told him you were bookin' in here. . . .'

Mann's face was blank, his grey eyes puzzled.

'Milburn, the clerk, is a cousin of mine and I asked him on the way up if Sievers had asked after you.'

'Why would you do that?'

'Well – I didn't care for the way he looked at me, very hard, cold. After he'd gone I recollected seein' him somewheres before, besides on his visits to town. It was on a Wanted dodger. An old one. It was for assault on some nester and his family – Yellow Peak, way, as I recollect.'

Mann stared silently.

'Well, he just looked mean today, almost on the prod. I figured mebbe you should know he's takin' an interest in you. If I'm pokin' my nose in where I ain't oughta, I'm sorry—'

'That's OK. I'm obliged. Likely mistaken identity. I dunno him. I haven't got another dollar on me right now but if you like to look me up in the bar of the Last Ace after supper, I'll be glad to buy you a drink.'

'Well, thanks, Mr Mann, but I wasn't lookin' for no sorta reward. I just—'

'What's your name?'

'Kelly, but, b'lieve it or not, most folk just call me "Hoss".'

'Wonder why?'

The stable man grinned and Mann took his gear from him and closed the door.

He leaned against it, flipped the burlap off the rifle and decided he would clean and oil it – and load it – after he'd had the hot bath he had ordered when he registered. Then he'd do the same to his Colt.

*

Hoss Kelly picked up his shot of whiskey from the sloppy bar top, briefly saluted Jubal Mann, who was bathed and shaved, dressed in clean but wrinkled clothes.

'Won't say "Mud in your eye", like some of them Limeys do. It could happen too easy on a night like this! But here's luck, anyway.'

Mann smiled and they threw down the burning spirits, quickly followed by a long draught of their frothing beers.

'Could polish brass with that whiskey.'

'If you don't mind the brass gettin' eaten away,' agreed the hostler. 'Say, that's a big roan you ride, but then you're a big man. What is he? Sixteen, seventeen hands?'

' 'Bout midway between. Carried me a lot of miles, old Tiny.'

'Tiny! You got a sense of humour!'

'I didn't name him. Kid belonging to the feller I bought him off called him that when he was little – the kid – *and* the roan. What's up?'

Jubal Mann asked the latter as he saw Hoss's face tighten and the man straightened quickly. 'Comin' up on you!'

Mann turned fast and found himself face to face with the large bearded man who had almost ridden him down in the livery entrance – Sievers. He jostled aside a couple of drinkers beside Mann now, ignored their glares, and said, 'You damn well spooked my hoss, mister, steppin' in front of him the way you did.' The voice was rough and loud and a wave of silence washed slowly along the bar, drinkers turning to see who was speaking.

'Spooked your *hoss*? Man, it's just as well it was rainin' so hard and my trousers were already wet or you'd've seen me soak 'em through, the way you charged in and spooked *me*!'

That brought a few chuckles but the bearded man scowled. 'You sassin' me?' Mann said nothing and the other, impatient, straightened to his full height – a couple of inches over Mann – and said, 'I asked was you sassin' me?'

Mann lifted a finger. 'Thinking about that, yeah! I guess I was.'

The silence was complete throughout the barroom now, the hiss of rain on roof shingles and storefronts easily audible. The bearded man stepped away from the bar, one hand crooked above the butt of his six-gun. The barkeep suddenly lifted a sawed-off Greener on to the counter.

'You know better'n that, Sievers!' He was a wide-shouldered man with a battered face and met the bearded man's glare stolidly. 'I've told you before – no guns in here.'

Sievers curled a lip and swung his gaze back to Mann. Hoss Kelly had moved along the bar a few spaces when he saw how this was shaping up. But Jubal Mann continued to stare at the bearded man, lifted his beer and drank. Sievers lunged, slapping at the big, heavy-based glass mug.

Jubal, ready for the move, stepped back quickly and the gnarled hand whistled past his face. He tossed the remaining beer into Sievers's eyes and as the man clawed at them, bounced the heavy glass off his head.

Sievers's hat was knocked askew and his legs buckled part-way as he clawed at the bar, got a grip and remained on his feet. Mann arched his eyebrows, staring at the unbroken glass mug. 'You must have a thick head, mister. Guess I should've figured that when you came in here on the prod.'

'I'll show you a damn thick – *fist*!'

Sievers swung a short right that Mann wasn't fast enough to dodge. It cracked against his jaw and he was hurled back along the bar, dropping the glass mug, arms flying wide to gain balance and knocking Hoss and another man sprawling. He went down himself when he reached the end of the counter.

By that time the bearded man was roaring in on him, stomping at his falling body.

The silence was broken now by a lot of yelling and cat-calling, men urging on the fighters. Mann's head was ringing and his face felt all lopsided, but he could still react. He dodged the boot that had been aimed at his belly, swung aside, then, unexpectedly, back again, catching the muddy boot in both hands.

He wrenched hard and Sievers yelled as he hopped on one leg, trying to keep balance. Mann swung the tree trunk leg savagely against the bar front and the bearded man yelled, staggered, his knee throbbing. Mann's fists were waiting. As the big, hairy face ducked down, Mann stepped forward, and, almost chest-to-chest with his opponent, hammered a barrage of blows into the other's midriff with the speed of a Gatling gun. Sievers was sent staggering back along the bar, one wildly-swinging arm knocking glasses and bottles flying. His big body cannoned into a trio of yelling cowboys, scattering them, one man falling.

The other two grabbed his arms and flung him back towards the advancing Jubal Mann. Three fast straight lefts jerked Sievers's head as if he were bouncing on his back down a flight of stairs. Then a looping right smashed his mouth, and again rammed in and bent the already battered nose.

Sievers went down almost all the way, one hand instinctively reaching up to grab at the bar's edge. He managed a grip and heaved himself up.

Mann was moving in and caught a boot in the belly. He jackknifed violently. Sievers's stained teeth showed through the beard as he bulled forward, turning a shoulder into Mann's face. He tasted blood, slammed back against the bar, his spine creaking painfully. Sievers reared above him and hammered a blow into his chest. It was like the kick from an army mule. The room spun into a red mist, swirled around and, after another two jarring blows, settled down, with Mann on the floor, his mouth half full of sawdust. He spat and blinked, wrenched his head around as Sievers grinned through his bloody beard. The big man growled hoarsely: 'Well I sure had to work at it, but the bounty's all mine, you son of a *bitch*!'

Even as the iron-hard knuckles sped towards his

face, Mann wrenched aside, felt the blow skid across his right shoulder, jarring his neck. Then Sievers yelled as his fist punched a hole in the woodwork of the bar front. He pulled and twisted to get his hand free, splinters tearing the flesh. Mann got his feet under him, kicked Sievers in the side and twisted fingers in the sweaty hair. He slammed the bloody face into the woodwork, then flung Sievers away from the bar, the man's hand bleeding profusely now. Mann reached for the front of the torn shirt and heaved him up against the counter.

He stepped back slightly, took time to drag down a deep, though painful, breath and put his shoulders behind a looping punch. The connecting *crack!* echoed across the smoke-filled room. Sievers's head snapped around and his body followed, rolling a few feet along the bar. But his legs couldn't support him and he sprawled face down on the floor, moaning, moving feebly.

Mann was bent almost double, gasping for breath, shaking his sore right hand. Then Hoss Kelly took his arm and guided him to the bar where the ugly barkeep pushed a slopping glass of whiskey towards him.

'On the house,' he said, deadpan. 'You've earned it.'

The deputy took his job too damn seriously for Mann's liking.

His name was Barnes and he worked full time as deputy to the sheriff, a man of some reputation in the law business, called Luke Gower. Mann had heard of him as far out as California, and wondered if he was going to get out of this just on a 'disturbing the peace' charge. Deputy Barnes said he could find himself in more serious trouble.

Sievers was in a back room, having his broken nose packed with ribbon bandage by a sawbones, and his maimed hand tended to. Mann, tired of Barnes probing questions, said, 'Why don't you go bother Sievers? He started it – ask anyone who was at the bar at the time.'

'Already have,' Barnes told him. He was a medium tall man, wide of shoulder and waist, with a hard face that reminded Mann of a Top Sergeant he had once encountered during the War. 'Thing I'm interested in, mister, is that a dozen men heard Sievers say, he'd earned himself the bounty that's on your head.'

'I dunno what he was talking about – I've got no bounty on me. Go check your Wanted dodgers. You won't find any with my name on 'em.'

'Mebbe you're there under another name.'

'Judas priest! Why the hell're you hassling me? I've already told you I'm a cattle buyer and here—'

'You couldn't give me the name of a ranch or Association you're buyin' for.'

'Because I work for myself. I'm a freelance! You know what that means?'

'Don't push it, Mann!'

Jubal sighed and shook his head. 'Look, the owner of the Double Bar K in the Texas Panhandle, Lee Kennedy, said he'd be interested sometime to see what kinda steer you'd get if you crossed a longhorn with one of these Wyoming beef cattle you got up here, known for their meat. "Carcass-quality", they call it. I was headed up this way and figured why not buy a couple good-blood stud steers – about all I could afford – and take 'em back with me, sell 'em to Kennedy or let him try 'em out, me taking a percentage of any sales he made.'

'Risky, ain't it?'

Mann shrugged. 'If it pays off, I'll be in on the start of a whole new breed, and it'll be a seller's market.'

Deputy Barnes made yet another note in his book and frowned as he looked up at Mann. Hoss Kelly spoke up.

'Hell, Link, Sievers has been in trouble before. He had no cause to prod Mr Mann, just bein' ornery. I've seen him once or twice over the last few months, always hasslin'. Pidge Morton told me he did time for some trouble in Deadwood once. Whyn't you give Mann a break?'

Barnes glared. 'You'd be wise to mind your business, Hoss. I'll get round to Sievers. Meantime, Mann, you come on down to the law office and meet our sheriff. I reckon he'll be mighty interested in you.'

'You can bet it'll be more than I'm interested in him,' Mann said, dabbing at his bleeding mouth.

'Wait here while I go collect Sievers. Sheriff can question you both at the same time.'

Mann swore and picked up his battered hat, jamming it hard on his thick cap of brown hair. 'I'm gettin' the hell outta here,' he murmured as the deputy made for the back room where Sievers was getting medical attention.

Hoss Kelly grabbed his arm quickly. 'Hell, Jubal, don't do that! They'll have a posse on your neck before you can clear town!' Mann hesitated and Hoss added, 'Anyway, you got nothin' to worry about have you? You said there's no bounty on you, no dodgers. . . . Stick around and let 'em get it over with. Better'n high-tailin' it and having Luke Gower comin' after you. He never gives up.'

Mann frowned. He dabbed again at his bleeding lip and by then the deputy was coming out of the back room with Sievers, who had a heavy bandage over his broken nose.

Too late now! He'd have to square up to the law. *Goddamnit!*

CHAPTER 2

THE BOUNTY

Sheriff Luke Gower was a rail-lean, hard-bitten lawman whose long, violent years in the job showed in the craggy face and the steely eyes. He was older than Mann had thought – in his fifties – but he still looked mighty hard and no-nonsense, though there was a kind of built-in weariness now in his manner.

He glanced up from Link Barnes's notebook, studying Mann for several moments of unnerving silence.

'Seem to know your name, Mann.'

The sheriff waited but Jubal Mann said nothing.

'I'll look through my Wanted dodgers – got me a heap.' His lips twisted in a mirthless smile 'Bout three hundred at last count, from all over the country.' He flicked his gaze to the sober-faced Barnes. 'Think we could make Mr Mann comfortable for a few hours, mebbe overnight, Link?'

'Still got a couple cells vacant, Luke. 'Course I ain't made a full town patrol yet, so he might have to double up with a few drunks.'

'Now wait up!' snapped Mann, feeling irritated by some of his bruises and swellings, as well as this harassment. His words were slurred because of his swollen jaw and he winced as he rubbed it gently. 'You got no call to lock me up. Goddammit, I never started the fight. What're you doin' about Sievers?'

'Mr Sievers is sleeping it off in one of our cells right now,' Gower told him calmly. 'We've dealt with him before and know he's a troublemaker.'

'Then why the hell am I. . . ?' Mann paused. 'I get it – that "bounty" thing! I dunno where Sievers got the notion there's a bounty on me. I'm not a wanted man. You can look from now 'til Doomsday and you won't find a dodger with my name on it.'

Gower tapped a pencil on the edge of the desk. 'You could be tellin' the truth – as you know it.'

'It *is* the truth! As I know it or anyone else does.'

Gower flicked out one finger; it was a command for silence and a shadow touched his eyes as they pinched down slightly. Mann figured it was prudent to shut up.

'Won't take me long to look through them dodgers, figure two, three hours to check over the last couple years. That ought to be far enough back. It don't seem longer'n that since I reckon I heard your name. You're a Texan, ain't you?'

Mann hesitated, shook his head. 'Missouri – family moved to Texas when I was just a shaver.'

'They still there?'

Mann's face tightened. 'Yeah – all buried in Texas sod.' Both lawmen tensed and looked at him more sharply.

'The war?' asked the sheriff.

'Comanche massacre – I'm the last Mann.'

'In more ways than one,' murmured Link Barnes.

Gower frowned, gaze hard and penetrating. 'You survived?'

'Wasn't there. I . . . run out when I was sixteen. Mad to fight the Yankees. Pa said I was needed on that hardrock spread he was trying to build-up but I couldn't see it happenin', and we argued and I . . . left.'

Barnes snorted but Gower studied Mann very closely. 'And still regret it like hell.'

Jubal Mann straightened a little, meeting Gower's challenging stare. 'I've regretted it since I got the news about the massacre – in the middle of the battle at Shiloh.'

'You were in that!' Barnes exclaimed. 'Judas – you're a born survivor then, Mann! Missed the massacre of your family and lived through one of the bloodiest battles of the War.'

Gower held up a hand and frowned at his deputy. 'I'm inclined to believe you, Mann, but I need to know somethin' of what you've been doin' since the war ended. Link, put him in that end cell – no one there right now – and get the diner to send him in some supper.'

'I'd as soon eat it in the damn diner! Or a hog

pen, come to that.'

'You interest me, Mann, so you'll stay with us for a spell.' Gower jerked his head at Barnes. The deputy touched Mann's shoulder and Jubal sighed resignedly and got to his feet. The deputy took his right arm and led him through the doorway to the cell block. . . .

Gower pursed his lips, then rose and went to a cupboard. He opened it and stared at the shelves packed with ragged, musty Wanted dodgers.

Hell, there were more than he remembered!

But he had to be sure. Luckily he had them divided state by state, but there was a daunting number just the same. Grunting a little, he fumbled out a foot-thick pile and turned back to his desk with them, yelling, 'Link! Get in here.'

The damn over-zealous deputy had started this. Now he could damn well help out, between town patrols.

The greasy supper from the nearby diner didn't set easy in Jubal Mann's belly. He was sore there from a kick Sievers had given him and his other aches and pains from the fight wouldn't allow him to sleep properly – a series of cat-naps was all he could manage.

So when the ruckus started just after midnight, he was already half awake.

There was shouting at first – urgent panicky voices – followed by several gunshots. Despite his headache and stiffening muscles, he jumped up on the bunk and stretched up to the bars of the window.

Already he could see a small reddish glow against the night sky. If it was a fire – in a mostly clapboard town! – there would be many curses now because the earlier deluge had ended at least two hours ago. *Nature had a queer sense of humour . . . and timing. . . .*

There was a clanging bell, ringing the call for the volunteers of the Cheyenne Fire Department. More noise, endless shouting, the crash of breaking furniture, likely being thrown out of upper floor windows to save it from the flames, but busting it all to hell dropping into the street from that height.

Horses were whinnying and he heard the rumble of wheels, the swearing of men as the horse-drawn fire wagon bogged down in the mud.

'Shoulders!' a deep voice bellowed. 'Get your goddamn *shoulders* into it or the Regal'll be nothin' but a pile of ash by the time we get there. *Heave*, you sons of. . . .'

The Regal Hotel! Damn! He hoped his gear wouldn't get burned up!

'Hey!' he yelled through the bars. 'What's happening out there?'

'Shut up an' let a man get some sleep, you son of a bitch!' The angry voice came from one of the other darkened cells. Another backed up the first man's sentiments and Mann jumped as high as he could, grabbing the bars and pulling himself up until his face was against two of the cold, rust-flaked rods. It hurt his bruised face to strain against the iron as he twisted his neck, trying to see. He glimpsed the gleaming brass on the fire wagon as they finally got it unbogged but then it turned a corner and he lost sight. He did see a crowd surging after it, though.

The fire was blazing high now, throwing flickering light over the buildings, columns of sparks lifting to rival the stars that were trying to peek through the scudding rain clouds.

Mann couldn't hold his weight for long and lowered himself down to the bunk, none the wiser about the cause of the ruckus – except that there was a fire burning merrily one block over where he had his room in the Regal.

But what was the gunfire earlier. . . ?

He found out a couple of hours later, wakened from a half-sleep by Deputy Barnes, kicking the underneath of the bunk mattress, boot toe jarring Mann's aching body on top.

'Up! Up! Come on awake, you! Sheriff wants you in the front office!'

'Keep the goddamn noise down!' some drink-slurred voice bawled from the cell next door. Others chorused and cursed the deputy who seemed to be in a bad mood.

'Shut up, you moanin' bastards, or I'll get the fire hose turned on you!'

He shoved and nudged Mann all the way through to the front office where a haggard-looking Gower sat at his desk. Both lawmen smelled of smoke. The sheriff glanced up with reddened eyes, though they still looked menacing. He gestured to a straightback chair and Mann dropped into it, scrubbing a hand – *gently!* – down his swollen and bruised face.

'The hell's all the excitement, Sheriff?'

Gower stared at him in silence for a long time then said, 'I think you're the cause of it.'

Mann sat back in the chair, frowning. 'Me? How the hell? I've been in that lousy cell for—'

'Shut up,' Gower told him wearily. 'I've got a goddamn headache that'd drop a bull buffalo and it's gettin' worse.' He tapped dirty, blistered fingers on his desktop. 'Tad Milburn, the clerk at the Regal, heard we'd locked you up for the night. So when some trail-weary, half-drowned parson staggered into the foyer, looking for a room, he rented out yours.'

'Greedy sonuver.'

'As mebbe. But – a *parson*! Man of the cloth, man of God, if you like – no one you'd expect to be the target of an assassin.'

Mann went very still, started to speak, but remained silent. Gower clenched a fist and slammed it down hard on his desk, making a heavy glass inkwell and a pen set jump.

'Someone – *someone* – on the veranda outside your room, kicked in the window, threw in a lighted lamp which, naturally, broke and set the carpet on fire. The parson jumped out of bed and that someone at the window pumped three shots into him. Leastways, we think it was only three. Kind of hard to tell, the way those flames cooked him.'

'Jesus!' Then Mann stiffened. 'It could've been me! That what you're saying?'

'*Exactly* what I'm saying! And I'm adding this: *if* there is a bounty out on you, it looks like it'll be paid – dead or alive. You have any thoughts about that?'

Mann shook his head almost absently, frowning, mind in a swirl. 'There's gotta be some mistake.'

'That the best you can do?'

'Goddammit, sheriff, I'm just as puzzled as you are! *I'm not a wanted man!*'

Gower smiled crookedly. 'Mebbe not by the law – but someone wants you bad enough to slap a price on your head.'

Mann remained silent, consciously composing his battered face, trying to keep it blank. 'I don't have any enemies who'd do that.'

'Mr Cleanskin, huh?' suggested Barnes sardonically.

'Hell, I've had my troubles, but nothin' – *nothin'* – I can think of to explain this. Someone must have me mixed up with someone else. What happened to the feller who killed the parson, anyway?'

Gower swung his gaze to Barnes who said, tersely, 'He tried to run, started shootin' – I brought him down. But he died while the sawbones was tendin' him.'

'Say anything first?'

Barnes shook his head. 'Drifter. Panhandled a local ranch before hittin' town. Told someone in the bar he was a bounty hunter – that word again!' He paused, looking expectantly at Mann who remained silent and deadpan. 'I figure you've got a heap of trouble, Mann, if you can't come up with an explanation.'

The ball was deftly thrown back into Jubal's lap and he shook his head vigorously. 'Hell, I've been tryin' to tell you I can't think of. . . .'

His voice trailed off and Gower leaned forward quickly. 'You just think of somethin'?'

He had to ask the question again and Mann kind of shook himself and said, 'No – just running through my head most of the big troubles I've had. . . . Hell, the biggest'd be durin' the war, I guess. . . .'

He paused and both men waited, impatience on their hard faces. Gower snapped, 'Tell it, damn you!'

'We-ell, some gal in Kingman, Kansas, had her heart set on me, and – she got pregnant. Or said she did. Her father and three brothers come after me. They laid it on the line: marry her or die. They meant it. Strict, Bible-bangin' Methodists. The Old Man was so loco about his daughter bein' de-flowered he couldn't see he'd be committin' a bigger sin if he did kill me. The brothers would do whatever he said, of course. Anyway, I managed to get away and I rode a hundred miles and still there was a dust cloud behind me. I was only a kid, seventeen, and scared silly, so I went and joined the army.' He spread his hands as the others waited for more.

'You think the girl's father might still be harbourin' a grudge and. . . ?'

'Hell, I dunno. He wouldn't have that kind of money. Sank it all into his church – he was a lay-preacher. Still likely askin' forgiveness for even thinking about killing me – if he's still livin'.'

The lawmen continued to stare but Mann said nothing more. *He'd been setting out on a chore to blow some tree stumps when they had come after him, and had some dynamite in his saddle-bags. When they started shooting and he was winged in an arm by a ricochet, he planted the dynamite in a narrow cutting. Not used to handling explosives, he cut the fuses too short and the explosion was early, sent tons of earth and rock down into the cutting, on top of the pursuers. He was sure at least two of them had been killed, but didn't wait around to check. The panic stayed with him all the way to the recruiting office where, in case he was now wanted for murder, he joined the army under the name of Ruben Beck . . . to be on the safe side.*

He could see that something was bothering the sheriff. Barnes would simply go along with whatever Gower decided. The sheriff said carefully, 'This don't go with your story about runnin' away from home like you told us: couldn't wait to start killin' Yankees, that right?'

'I'd already run. Lost my urge to join the army for a spell and I'd earned a few bucks cuttin' railroad ties. Decided to have a wingding first: that's when I met the gal.'

'Mmmmm. Then there's another angle: you said you'd got together some money for buyin' stud bulls. They don't come cheap. You think someone knows about it and is after your cash?'

'No cash, it's all in a bank warrant. And that's sitting in the safe at the Cheyenne Branch of the Wyoming First National. I'll call on it when I need it. No sense in carryin' all that *dinero* around.'

'How much?' asked Barnes and Mann swivelled his gaze to the hard face.

'A few thousand.' Mann's tone was clipped.

'How'd you come by that much?' Barnes demanded.

It seemed Mann wasn't going to answer but then he said: 'I've just come up from Creede, Colorado – worked the Cherry Creek goldfields and hit a tolerably rich vein. I—'

He paused as Gower suddenly snapped his fingers and leaned across the desk. '*That's* where I've heard your name! There was a deal of claim-jumping going on down there, right?'

Face tight now, Mann nodded warily.

'Bunch of vigilante miners finally got together, ratted out the robbers and strung up three of 'em on the spot.' Mann remained silent under Gower's stare. 'You were one of the vigilante ring-leaders. . . .' Still only silence from Mann. 'You must've made a lot of enemies there.'

'Lot of friends, too. That was months ago, Sheriff. There's no bounty on me for that.'

'Should've been! You broke the law! I got no time for anyone takes the law into his own hands.'

'Then you've never had money you've busted your back for stolen by some stinkin' thief who figures he's more entitled to it than you. I was working a claim on my own and that was bad enough. But I had friends on the field who were married, had families to support: they were robbed blind just the same, without hesitation, left without a red cent. Sure, I led the vigilantes. And I'd do it again.'

'Not in my town – not that there's any chance you'd need to – but you're trouble with a capital "T", Mann. I don't want you here. Come daylight, you clear Cheyenne.'

'I need to see the banker about my warrant.'

'You heard!' snapped Link Barnes, jaw thrusting.

Gower lifted a hand slightly. 'Easy, Link. All right, Mann. Bank opens at nine thirty – you be gone by ten.'

Stiffly, Jubal Mann climbed to his feet. 'Think I'd've been better off if I'd lost that fight.'

Gower gave him a crooked smile. 'You win some, lose some. Ain't you learned that yet?'

'Mebbe. An' sometimes I'm a bad loser.'

Gower scowled, jerked a thumb at Barnes.

'Get him outta here, Link.'

CHAPTER 3

HALF-MOON PASS

The air was clean as a knife cut after the rain and Cheyenne steamed and sweated as the streets dried out under the scorching sun.

Jubal Mann attended to his business at the bank, arranging that he would send a password by telegraph when he wanted the warrant transferred to another bank or a cattle agency, if he could do a deal. He withdrew twenty-five dollars in cash and slogged his way through the swampy streets to Liddel's General Store. Here he bought new clothes – Mr Lidell allowed him to change into them in a back store room – and he found a pair of boots he liked that fitted well enough, although they were a mite tight if he wore thick woollen socks.

But he had long been used to wearing no socks and refused when the storekeeper offered him a set of nickel-plated spurs at a discount.

'Don't use spurs, neither.'

Lidell, a moustached, pudding of a man, arched his bushy eyebrows. 'I admire a man who considers his horse, sir.'

'Loco not to. He's got to carry you to where you want to go.'

'And might I ask where you're headed now, young feller?'

Mann levelled his stare, then smiled faintly. 'In a northerly direction, maybe even north-west.'

Liddell smiled. 'Good enough! But if you aim to go westerly, take Half-Moon Pass through the Tall Men – that's a range of hills still got a snow cap at this time of year. Save you many miles and a long climb, that pass.'

'Obliged, storekeeper. Guess I'll have three cartons of them .44/.40 bullets, too.'

Liddell's smile pulled in at the edges slightly, but he nodded affably enough and reached up for the ammunition.

'I hope you won't have to use 'em up.'

'Me too. Better throw in a bottle of gun oil and some bore-cleanin' patches.'

'I believe I see here a man who cares for his guns, as well as his horse.'

'Be a fool not to.'

'Wish you good luck, sir.'

'Thanks – I can use some.'

And when he picked up his sorrel at the livery, Mann felt more than ever he needed all the luck he could get.

Hoss Kelly handed over the reins and watched silently as Mann stashed his parcels in his saddle-bags and swung easily aboard the well-groomed roan.

'You hear Gower turned Sievers loose?'

Mann checked as he lifted the reins, shook his head.

'Judge fined him and he had to pay for the wrecked chairs in the saloon, then Gower kicked him outta town.'

'See which way he went?'

'Same trail as you'll be takin'. He could even swing off to Half-Moon Pass. . . . Keep your eyes open, Jubal.'

'I'll do that. Say, you know anything about the *hombre* killed the parson? Gower figures he must've thought it was me, after this damn "bounty" they keep talkin' about.'

Hoss arched his eyebrows and pursed his lips. 'Well, mebbe I can see it that way, too. No, I never seen the feller Barnes shot down. But Mr Pendelton, from the Bar P Slash, was in. He said the feller stopped off and cadged a meal and they let him replace a broken shoe on his hoss, before headin' into Cheyenne. Called himself Kelty. Mentioned he was from Laramie way, had a lead on a feller with a bounty he was after. He must've meant you.'

'Seems that way. Much obliged for everything, Hoss.'

They shook hands and Mann rode out through the livery doors, figuring to stop somewhere safe along the way and tend to his guns. Just in case.

It was much colder at night in the hills and he built a good fire in front of a flat rock so that it reflected heat across his bedroll. He let it burn down to coals and threw on a handful of semi-green sticks. They smoked a good deal but would catch fire eventually. The small smoke screen helped mask his next movements, should there be anyone watching out there in the mountain night.

He had his warbag all set up, rolled and strapped, slid it under the blanket and stuffed his old boots at one end, his hat at the other. Then, bellied down, he slid into the shadow and behind the rock where he had left his rifle – newly cleaned and oiled, with a full magazine.

He shivered some and pulled his new corduroy jacket tighter, buttoning up some of the brass buttons. His hands tingled as he touched the rifle's metal parts and his head felt cold. For many years he had subscribed to the range-rider's habit of hat-off last thing at night, hat-on first thing in the morning. He had learned it in the army, too, and wished he was wearing his curlbrim right now.

But it was being used for another chore this night.

Time passed and he had to fight to stay awake.

Then he heard the crunch of gravel under a boot, maybe on the ground or as a man climbed on to a rock so as to get above the camp. Between two rocks he could see the fire's coals throwing a ruddy light on his bedroll, bright enough to show boots and hat and the suggestive detail of a sleeping man under the blanket.

A movement caught his eye to the left and he swung that way in time to see a man down on one knee atop a flat rock, rifle to shoulder. He heard the snap of the lever jacking a shell into the breech, followed swiftly by the gunshot. The lead thunked into the warbag beneath the blanket and was followed by three more deliberate shots. His hat flew into the clearing and he had time to curse because there would be a bullet hole in it now – but better that *he* wasn't in it. . . .

'Told you I'd get that bounty, Mann!' Sievers's harsh voice crowed as he stood up, the smoking rifle down at his right side now.

Mann stood, too, his Winchester held in both hands. 'Knew you'd turn out to be a back-shooter, Sievers.'

The killer spun so fast he almost lost footing but he had his wits about him. He jumped down into the campsite from the rock as Mann fired. The bullet ricocheted from the flat rock and Sievers was belly down and rolling, rifle arcing around to spit fire at the sound of Mann's voice.

Jubal dropped between the rocks. The lead snarled above him, showering him with grit. He squirmed forward and instinctively ducked as two more shots hammered. He twisted on to one side, slid under the curve of a big boulder and found a small triangle of clear space in front of his face.

He aimed and triggered, working the lever swiftly,

got off his second bullet so close to the first that it might have been mistaken for a single shot. He heard Sievers grunt and the man reared, half erect, and dived behind a low rock.

Even as he was in mid-air, only for a brief second or two, Mann stood and braced his rifle butt against his right hip, working lever and trigger in a blur. The short, hammering volley hurt his ears, enclosed by rocks as he was in this position, and the roar drowned any cry Sievers may have made as his heavy form was spun this way and that by striking lead.

The big, bearded bushwhacker was down, his rifle stock shattered by one of Mann's bullets, body bleeding from multiple wounds.

Jubal could hear the blood bubbling in the back of the man's throat as he crossed warily, his last live round in the breech, thumb holding back the hammer, trigger depressed. All he had to do in case of danger was lift his thumb enough to allow the hammer to fall and the weapon would discharge.

But Sievers wasn't going to give him any trouble.

The big man had three of Mann's bullets in him and the way he was gasping for air so wetly, blood trickling from his mouth, Mann figured his lungs had been torn up. He squatted, pulled the man's neckerchief off and wiped blood from the bearded face and mouth.

'No bounty, Sievers. Who is it wants me dead so badly, anyway?'

There was only a bubbling sound and Mann wiped away a thick stream of fresh blood from Sievers's mouth. 'Nothin' I can do for you, Sievers. I'll bury you decent before I move on, whether you talk or not: that's all I can promise you. But I'd sure as hell like to know who's willing to pay for someone to kill me. How much, too.'

Sievers was looking up at him with eyes that were full of fear and pain. He groped feebly for Mann's hand, touched his wrist. He made a series of half-spitting sounds and Mann jerked back. He wasn't sure but the dying man might have said—

'Five thousand! Is that what you said?' Sievers nodded jerkily. 'Christ! Who'd want me dead that bad?'

He had to lean close. This time Sievers finished his brief words with a rattling cough that took him out of this world into whatever waited beyond his pain. . . .

Mann sat back on his hams, frowning, no longer noticing the cold of Half-Moon Pass.

'*Captain?*' he murmured. 'Captain who. . . ? Hell, I was no perfect soldier, but I know damn well I never riled no Captain so that he'd put up $5,000 to have me killed!'

Unless, after all, it had something to do with those brothers he thought might have died in the pass he had blown down. What the hell was their name again. . . ? Tomkin, that was it. Sherry Tomkin's kin. 'Aw, you turned out to be the Queen of Bitches, Sherry, my love, with that damn bewitching body of yours. . . !'

But the war had been over for nigh on seven years. It had been running for about a year when he had fled from the Tomkins and joined-up. *Hell almighty!*

That would make a total of twelve, thirteen years. Who the hell would hold a grudge, imagined or not, that long, and put up all that money just to see him dead? *Not even the hell-bitch Sherry. Her interest in any one man couldn't possibly last that long: she wasn't called The Bed-hopper for nothing. . . .*

No. It must be something else. A mistake! Yes!

There *had* to be some mistake – and the quicker he cleared it up, the better.

'And you can say that again!' he said out loud as he reloaded the rifle, before starting the unpleasant chore of digging a grave for Sievers.

But who the hell could it be?

And why. . . ?

Mann had heard of the Bar P Slash – it was rumoured that the 'slash' had only been added to the brand after Mrs Pendleton had run off with a Chicago meathouse agent who was heading back to the windy city.

Bryce Pendleton had a good reputation in the cattle business for producing prime beef and was able to command high prices for his herds. Someone had told Mann that Pendleton always maintained his cows were well served by bulls that came from a British Colony in the South Pacific called Australia: a dumping ground for convicts after they lost the American colonies. Which probably meant the bulls had originated in England or India or some other part of the British Empire before being taken to this raw new land.

He had been lucky enough to be in Baltimore on other business – searching for the future (and temporary) Mrs Pendleton, in fact – when a storm-battered lime juicer had limped into port, under jury-rig, main-mast and mizzen gone, along with half the starboard rail and a third of the crew, and offloaded what remained of her cargo.

A hundred cattle bound for some British possession in the Caribbean had been sent ashore, sick, some injured, most of which were put down – but with six prime Red Angus bulls that had escaped serious injury in the hurricane.

The harassed captain wanted cash fast and agreed to a ridiculously low price – to Pendleton's real surprise – and he hurriedly went to the nearest branch of his bank, paid cash-on-the-barrelhead and the bulls were his.

He had friends in Baltimore and was able to rest his purchases on the well-grassed acres of one man's estate, allowing them to regain their health before he shipped them out to his growing cattle ranch outside of Cheyenne.

Mann had intended to approach Pendleton with his idea of the new breed he was contemplating. So when, the day after burying Sievers, he traversed the remains of Half-Moon Pass and saw a signpost with several crude planks nailed to it, and one of them pointed north-west with the Bar P Slash brand burned into it, he figured his luck must be holding.

Pendleton had talked with the man who had mistakenly killed the parson in the Regal, too. It could be he would learn something that might help him figure out why he had become a clay pigeon for men with itchy trigger fingers, after easy money.

He was on the dodge, literally running for his life – and he didn't even know why.

CHAPTER 4

THE RED
ANGUS DEAL

Bryce Pendleton looked as prosperous as his ranch, which sprawled across rolling hills as well as many acres of meadows where the grass undulated like waves of an inland sea.

There were islands of colour in that sea of grass, some broad in area where the cattle had bunched around a particularly juicy patch, or in smaller, isolated dots as single animals chose their own feeding site.

But, even sitting his roan on top of the rise south of the big sprawling ranch house, Mann could pick out the Red Angus bulls – he counted seven, though one he wasn't sure of. It could have been a belted Angus, or even a Galloway.

'Must be bull heaven out there,' he opined.

Straddling a big black gelding with a wicked eye, Pendleton smiled. 'They are what you might call, "satisfied" with their harem. But it doesn't stop them using up any left-over energy in a head-butting contest every so often.'

'They gore each other?' Mann asked quickly.

Pendleton was a heavy-bodied man, not all that tall, but wide and thick through. He had a pleasant face with clear blue eyes that Jubal knew already could show a shrewdness in a flash – with a touch of steel around the edges. Here was a man who would never get the wrong end of a deal, or, if somehow he did, he would regret it for the rest of his life, trying to puzzle out how he had allowed it to happen.

'No goring,' he answered now in his pleasant voice. 'I won't allow them to harm each other. They know that.'

Mann wondered how a man, even a man of Pendleton's reputation, could control such huge animals – or could he? Those shrewd eyes were twinkling now and Mann suspected he was being ribbed. When the rancher's very white teeth showed as he threw back his head and laughed he knew he was right.

Going along with it, Mann said, 'What d'you do? Spank 'em?'

This time Pendleton guffawed, slapping a hand against one thick thigh. 'Man! Now that conjures up a picture! Spank 'em, by God! I'd sure like to see it happen – and the man foolish enough to try it.'

Jubal smiled. 'Well – it won't be *this* "Mann", I can tell you.'

Pendleton took out a tortoiseshell cigar case with silver frames and offered it to Mann. Jubal took one and when it was lit knew he had never tasted such rich, mellow, deeply satisfying tobacco. He savoured the smoke with each drag, before exhaling.

'You live well, Bryce.'

'I try to. Spent enough early years riding a grubline.' He gestured towards the grazing animals. 'Best thing I ever did was buy those Red Angus from that lime juicer in Baltimore. Might've been one of the first in the country to try them under our conditions – took a chance, mind, but it's paid off.'

'What makes 'em so good? Down south it's all longhorns. All you hear is how great they are.'

'And so they are, for that type of country. They have an enviable trait of being able to go long distances without adequate feed or water, even finding their own food on occasion. They can survive desert sun and winter snow, all excellent attributes for long trail drives, as you'd know.'

Mann nodded. 'Do I detect a slight Lone Star accent there? Not to mention a trace of Rebel pride?'

'You're damned astute! I worked with an Austrian language teacher – of all things! – for two years to cut that El Paso twang. Found it a hindrance in business up this way. Yes, I still have a very soft spot for longhorns. I'm mighty interested in your notion to try cross-breeding them with Red Angus. It could make a damned good combination.'

'Well, you say the Red Angus hide is good because the colour reflects the sunlight – something I never thought about before, but then I'm no expert breeder.'

'Well, the red hide gives that extra reflection and it's been proved that there's less eye canker, or sub-urned udders in their heifer progeny. No polled traits either, and a built-in vigour you would marvel at, plus top carcass quality, I tell you. I'm living proof that those things pay off.' He swept his arm around casually. 'See for yourself.'

'I see, all right – you think my idea is feasible?'

'I do – and I'd like to be involved.'

Mann tugged his left earlobe. 'Ah! Now we come to it. I don't have all that much to invest; I thought maybe if I bought one, maybe two bulls for a start. . . .'

'That'd be fine if you want to wait a few seasons to build up enough progeny for a breeders' association to be interested in backing you. They require a lot of proof, which means a lot of progeny to study closely. I figure you should start with at least three, maybe four bulls.'

Mann shook his head. 'Haven't got that much cash, I'm afraid. I'm working on a shoestring.'

'Well, you know I'm interested. Maybe we can do a deal.' Jubal raised his eyebrows, questioningly. 'If we can work the figures, maybe I can let you have an extra bull or two in exchange for some longhorns that I can experiment with up here myself.'

'Hell, that's a great idea, but I hope you haven't got the notion I have a ranch of my own?'

'I guess I was hoping you at least had a share in one, but—' Bryce Pendleton shrugged, waved a care-less hand. 'I still have contacts down there. Suppose I sell you two of my bulls and give you an extra one in exchange for a bunch of say six or eight longhorn heifers? You arrange shipping?'

When Mann's face suddenly straightened out at that last, Pendleton added with a wink: 'I happen to own shares in two or three railroads that come up this way. So, say we leave the shipping arrangements to me and we can work out percentages and costs after we get our programme underway.'

'I have to tell you, Bryce, this is way better than I ever dreamed of!'

'And that's why I'm willing to make these concessions, Jubal – I'm a dreamer, too. I'm at a point where I can afford to take a gamble, while you're betting your whole future on a scheme that seems sound enough to me. I like that in a man, checking the odds before commitment.' He lowered his voice. 'Like to think it's how I started.'

Mann grinned, just about speechless, and in the end just stuck out his right hand. Pendleton gripped it firmly. 'That about does it, then, except to seal it with some damn fine whiskey I've imported – so Irish you can taste the peat in it. Let's go back to the house and I'll prove it to you.'

The whiskey was as good as Pendleton claimed and as the man poured his second glass, Mann said, 'Can I switch to another subject for a few minutes?'

The rancher looked at him sharply then half smiled as he nodded. 'You'll be wanting to know about that fool Kelty who stopped off here to pan-handle a meal and the use of my forge.'

Mann nodded. 'Seems he figured it was me still using that room at the Regal. And on the way here, I was ambushed by a man called Sievers who was trying to kill me so he could claim the same damn bounty Kelty said he tried for.'

Pendleton frowned, serious now. 'I heard about this bounty – Kelty was quite talkative over the meal we gave him. He wasn't drinking this,' he held up his glass of pale amber whiskey, 'but I still gave him a good quality liquor and it loosened his tongue somewhat.'

'I'd sure like to know what he said, especially about who was paying the bounty.'

'He didn't elaborate on that – at least, didn't get down to specifics.' Pendleton's eyes had changed to a hard glint now as he watched Mann's face. 'What he did say was that it was a payback for something that happened more than ten years earlier.'

'Judas priest! Then it must've been something during the war after all.' At Pendleton's quizzical look, Mann told him about Sievers's last words and how he thought the man said there was a 'captain' behind the bounty. 'It's got me flummoxed, Bryce – I was only a kid when I joined up. I had my troubles in the army like everyone else but I never crossed anyone, private to captain, bad enough to hold a grudge all this time, and to want to pay it off by killin' me and offering a bounty for it.'

Pendleton tapped his sunbrowned fingers lightly against the glittering decanter.

'The word "captain" was mentioned, Jubal. Afraid I didn't pay much attention. Kelty was a rather crude type, and grew cruder with each sip of whiskey. I excused myself and only saw him again when he was leaving.'

'It's got me licked, Bryce, and not a little worried. Gettin' so I can't walk or ride without screwin' my head side to side all the time. A true pain in the neck.'

'I sympathize with you. I'll ride with you back to Cheyenne in case there's any trouble with Gower. He's a fine sheriff, but a damned hard case and stubborn as, well, as a longhorn! And it's been known to have to actually light a small fire under its belly when one of them has decided not to move.'

Mann dutifully smiled, glad Pendleton was going to accompany him back to Cheyenne.

Luke Gower might not like him returning – for any reason – after ordering him out. But even the tough sheriff would listen to a man of Pendleton's standing.

Gower listened to Pendleton, all right, concerning his new partnership with Mann, but when Jubal – doing the right thing – told him about Sievers's attempt on his life and the outcome, the sheriff sat up straight in his chair and Link Barnes, leaning on one wall stepped away, alert.

'You killed him?' the sheriff snapped.

'In self-defence.'

'You say,' murmured Barnes.

'All the bullets are in his chest – none in the back.'

Barnes looked sharply at Gower who held Mann's gaze steadily. 'You say you buried him?'

'I can show you where – you can dig him up if you want to check him out.'

Pendleton grimaced a little, spoke sharply. 'Surely that won't be necessary, Sheriff?' Gower was obviously considering it and the rancher added a touch of exasperation to his tone. 'Good grief, man, Jubal has been the target all along! There's proof that both men, Kelty and Sievers, believed this mysterious "captain" has put a bounty of some $5,000 on his head. A man has every right to defend himself.'

Gower agreed. 'But it could make him jumpy and decide to shoot first when he saw anyone he figured was gonna try to collect that bounty.'

'How the hell would I know?' snapped Mann. 'They don't give you an even break when they know money's going to be paid for you – dead or alive.'

'You don't know you're wanted dead.'

'Well, you could hardly say Kelty or Sievers tried to take him alive,' Pendleton pointed out.

Luke Gower didn't like it but he was a fair man underneath that hard exterior. He thought it over and nodded. 'All I can say is Mann's lucky he has you to stand up for him, Mr Pendleton.'

'And I wouldn't do that unless I believed him. All right, he's done the right thing by letting you know he had to come back to Cheyenne. I think we can go to the bank and attend to our main business now?'

Pendleton stood up and flicked an eyebrow at Mann who also stood. Neither Gower nor Barnes cared for the rancher's assumption that it was all right to leave, but there was little they could do about it.

'You conclude your business and then leave town again, Mann,' Gower said, looking steadily at Pendleton. 'You, of course, Mr Pendleton are free to stay or otherwise.'

The rancher glanced out the window. 'I should hope so, Sheriff, but it'll be dark in an hour or so.'

'That ought to give you plenty of time to do your business,' Gower said. 'Mann can leave as soon as it's done.'

'We won't argue with you, Sheriff, but this kind of attitude will surely be remembered when elections come due.'

Gower shrugged, spoke with a hard edge. 'I'll accept the will of the townsfolk, Mr Pendleton.'

The rancher grunted and he and Mann left, hurrying to reach the bank before it closed for the day.

'You believe him – about Sievers, I mean?' asked Barnes.

Gower heaved a sigh. 'Yeah, Mann's honest enough. But he attracts trouble like a magnet pulls in iron filings. You keep an eye on him and see he quits town when he leaves the bank.' As Barnes started out, the sheriff added, 'On second thoughts, let him have some supper first if he wants. Just make sure he leaves after. I'll decide what to do about Sievers's body later.'

Barnes nodded curtly and left.

On the way to the bank, Mann and Pendleton paused as they were passing the stage depot, looking at one wall which was papered with new, brightly-coloured posters.

'Looks like Cheyenne is in for a touch of culture,'

opined the rancher. 'That particular theatre troupe is very good – I saw them in Denver not long ago and last year, when I was visiting my sister in Salt Lake City.'

'*Saucy Shakespeare,*' read Mann, the words amongst various coloured figures of half-clad women and men with unbuttoned shirts, spilling glasses of wine as they tried to reach the women's trailing petticoats. All seemed to be having a good time. 'Not a lot of culture, I reckon!'

Pendleton chuckled. 'It's actually quite a smart way of getting The Bard's works across, the dialogue is tuned to the audience and I have to admit I enjoyed some deep belly laughter. That's the female star – Andrea – *An-dray-uh*, they pronounce it.' He touched a finger to a larger figure of a slim, laughing redhaired woman showing a good deal of cleavage. 'She's very popular – it's a wonder the poster hasn't been torn down. Most of them are souvenired by – er – admiring males. . . . She's very good. I'd recommend the show to anyone. In fact, I think I'll pay it another visit. Why don't you come and we could spend an evening on the town and— Oh, damnit! I forgot. Gower won't let you stay.'

Mann just nodded, and turned towards the bank building, Pendleton following.

'She looks a beauty, but I don't think I'll risk jail just to see her perform.'

'No. Well, let's see what Banker Truscott has to say about our deal. . . .'

The banker listened, called in his head accountant and they began to work out some figures. Mann was sweating some by the time they arrived at his contribution. But he was keen to follow this deal through now and figured he could just about make it and have a few dollars left over: very few.

The banker was obviously keen, too, and agreed to give some backing and a low rate of interest. While the signatures were drying on the contracts, he stood, a youngish man for his position – barely fifty – and loosened his starched collar, exhaling with relief.

'Why don't you gentlemen join me for dinner and we can round out the evening by going to see that theatre group – I hear they're pretty good. Will you come?'

'Glad to,' Pendleton said breezily, 'but Mann here has been ordered to leave town by Sheriff Gower as soon as his business here is completed.'

'Oh? Well, suppose his business wasn't *quite* completed and I needed Mr Mann's signature in the morning? He'll have to stay over – I'll arrange it with the sheriff,' he said confidently. 'We'll meet at the Pegasus restaurant in an hour?'

That was fine with them and they both booked rooms at the Gresham Hotel, whose business had more than doubled since the Regal had been partially destroyed in the fire caused by Kelty's bumbling efforts.

In his room, Mann stripped to the waist and washed in the hot water he had ordered. Dressed only in his trousers, he combed his wet hair, making a parting, then lathered his face and prepared to shave off his three-day stubble.

He had run the razor down the left side when

there was a knock on the door. Sighing, holding the razor in one hand, a towel in the other he crossed the room and opened it.

He felt himself freeze, briefly rising almost to his toes as he looked at the red-haired woman from the theatre poster – Andrea . . . *An-dray-uh.* . . .

She was dressed in a dark green dress with ivory piping and lace around the collar, a small hat not much bigger than a saucer canted slightly over her left eye and she clutched a green velvet purse in a white-gloved hand. A very handsome woman, he allowed, and her smile was dazzling.

'Mr Jubal Mann?' He nodded, aware he was staring like some yokel, and tried to look more welcoming. 'May I come in. . . ?'

'Sure, you sure can.' He stepped to one side, frowning as her smile suddenly faded and she stared at his hairless chest – and the dagger-like purple birthmark just above the arch of his ribs.

Her green eyes met his and they were no longer friendly.

'Who are you?' she snapped.

'Wh-what? I just told you – Jubal Mann.'

'Liar!'

He stepped back as she opened her purse and brought out a gleaming silver, over-and-under derringer. Her white-gloved thumb cocked the small hammer as she said, 'I asked who you really are! Now tell me – and quickly, or I'll shoot you! I want to know why you're impersonating my brother – and what's happened to him.'

CHAPTER 5

JUBAL

Damn! He'd known it had to happen sooner or later – but why now!

He was going to protest, but what was the use? If she really was Jubal's sister – and as far as he knew Jubal hadn't had a single kin left in the world – then nothing he could say would convince her he was actually Jubal Mann.

He wiped the lather off his face and closed the door after her. That derringer was waving around a bit, but there was a look of determination on her beautiful face. And the hammer was still cocked. She kept looking at his chest.

He tried a different kind of bluff. 'I understood Jubal's kin were all dead – and I never did hear him mention a sister called Andrea – *An-dray-uh* if you prefer.'

Her eyes narrowed and he thought they might

have filled with the beginning of tears at his admission. That small jaw firmed and her grip seemed to tighten on the gun. He held his breath. . . .

'I was always called "Andy". I had a twin brother, Hal, who I admired very much, wanted to be just like him, wished I'd been a boy. I dressed like a boy, talked Ma into keeping my hair cut short – it was straw-coloured at that time. I even tried to deepen my voice.' She gave a small, explosive laugh. 'Silly kid stuff.' She stopped abruptly. 'You answer my questions! Where is Jubal? And who're you?'

'My real name's John Mundy. I joined the army calling myself "Ruben Beck" and later, took Jubal's identity.' He paused, gave a half-smile. 'I keep on, I'll forget who I really am.' She was waiting, jaw firm, tense. 'I'm afraid Jubal's dead, Andy.'

She went very still and white; he thought she wasn't even breathing for a long minute. And the gun had stopped waving about. He could feel his heart slamming against his ribs.

'I-I felt he must be but when I heard about Jubal Mann in connection with that hotel fire and shooting I—' Her voice trailed off and there was a moment's pause. 'If you killed him, you wouldn't admit it, so I won't even ask that question, but I want to know how he died.' She couldn't quite control the tremor in her voice. 'And I want the truth!'

How! Lord, he remembered every detail, as if it had happened yesterday instead of almost ten years ago. He suddenly cleared his throat, keeping his eye on the gun. 'Would you like to sit down?' he gestured to a lone straightback chair. 'It'll take a little time.'

'Stop stalling!' she snapped and he saw now that she was quite young – about twenty, if that. 'I will sit on the edge of the bed. You use the chair *and tell me what I want to know!*'

He nodded, relathered his face and completed his shave in just a few swift strokes of the razor. Sitting in the chair, he flicked his gaze to his six-gun belt and holster hanging over the end of the bed, but she was much closer to it than he was. . . . He cleared his throat again and told her about Sherry Tomkin and her wild-eyed father and brothers.

He didn't pull any punches, admitted he'd set his sights on Sherry and deliberately lied to her, claiming his father was a rich rancher in Texas, whereas he was an orphan on the drift. Sherry was generous with her favours and when she knew she was pregnant, she named John Mundy as the father, seeing a good life for herself and the child.

His protests were of no avail to her father and brothers; in fact, his attempt to tell them that half the young post-puberty men in the county could be the father of the unborn child only made them madder. They tried to kill him on the spot and he was lucky that he knew how to handle a gun. He threw a chair at them and as they dodged, shot his way out, killing two of their horses and hightailing it into rough country. *He had never moved so fast in all his life!* They winged him in the left arm and were closing in again within hours when he remembered the dynamite in his saddle-bags: he was supposed to use it to blast some stumps for the railroad ganger he was working for at the time. . . .

Weaving and dodging, driving the hard-worked mount frantically, he managed to get ahead, climbed to a narrow pass. He sat on the rim and prepared his charges, half his attention on the dust cloud that was drawing nearer at an alarming rate. He clambered down the side of the pass a few feet and hung one-handed while he rammed the dynamite under jutting rocks that he figured he could blast loose to start a landslide, fill the pass and be rid of pursuit by the time they took the long way round.

But he knew little about handling dynamite and had to guess how long to make the fuses. He guessed wrong. . . .

He had to make several attempts to light them and by the time they began to sputter the hunters had ridden well into the pass below. One of the brothers spotted him and their rifles lifted, shooting to kill. Triggering a couple of wild shots, he threw himself over the rim, bullets clipping the edge only inches from him. He was never certain whether it was too-short fuses or if one of those ricocheting bullets hit a primed dynamite stick, but—

There was a sudden, ear-shattering explosion, streaks of fire and choking smoke. The blast picked him up bodily and hurled him ten feet back from the edge. Rocks and soil erupted and he covered his head with his arms as debris pattered down around him, some stones striking his body. Luckily they were small and when he peered tentatively over the broken, now crumbling rim, coughing in the dust of the roaring landslide, he saw one horse below, already down, half buried under a pile of rock and dirt, legs kicking feebly. The old man on the ground was sitting up, dazed, blood on his face. One of the others – he thought it was the youngest brother, Seth – was sprawled nearby, moving, groaning, but at least still alive. There was no sign of the other two, or their mounts. Then he heard the old man's cracked voice calling to his sons as he clawed feebly at some of the dirt and rocks, desperately trying to excavate. The young one staggered to help.

'*Luke! Buck!*' The old man's voice was cracked with anxiety. Realizing that digging was futile, he sat back and shook his fist at the broken rim where John Mundy crouched. 'You be dead, boy! Dead as my two fine sons you just buried here! As of this moment your life has *ended*. Curse you, for the murderin' snake you are!'

He palmed up his six-gun and started shooting, bullets flying wild and free as Mundy scrabbled back and staggered up to run for his mount.

The grief-cracked voice reached him clearly:

'I'll hunt you down if it takes the rest of my life, you son of a bitch! Vengeance shall be mine!'

It wasn't so much the threat that scared John Mundy but the sound of that voice: it was that of a madman, insane with grief, and he knew he would hear it in his dreams for a long, long time. *Dreams? They'd be damn nightmares!*

And they pursued him across a stretch of alkali

that nearly finished his horse and himself, too. But he reached water in time, climbed the refreshed mount up a knoll, and there, way back, negotiating the alkali, too, was the dust cloud he had been trying to throw for days.

Belly knotted, he spurred down the far side of the knoll and that sundown, saw lights far ahead from the saddle of his near-jaded mount. He made a cold, hidden camp, rose before sunup, headed in the right direction and found Fort McLeary, where the army was desperate for new men as the war got into full stride. He was pronounced fit and accepted within minutes of declaring his intention of fighting for the Confederacy. When asked his name, realizing that the Tomkins knew him as John Mundy, he signed *Ruben Beck* (made it up on the spot) on his enlistment form.

He was not yet seventeen, and within days had met another young man about the same age, Jubal Mann. They had only two days' 'training' and then were ordered into the bloody terror of the battlegrounds – the 'Killing Fields' as some reporter for one of the big Eastern papers christened them; hurled into gunsmoke and blood and thunder as the Yankees swept south. They were places of slaughter and horror and Jubal and Mundy consoled each other, badly affected by the sight of maimed and broken men, body parts strewn across the countryside. At one place under a long siege, called Bracken's Folly – sure *someone's* folly, anyway – the dead had been hastily buried in shallow graves. When the siege showed no signs of letting up, survivors were ordered to dig in, shelter in a series of zigzag trenches. It was fine, until one meal-time – a rare thing, to be fed, when a putrid, skeletal arm suddenly fell out of the trench wall and landed across the lap of a soldier eating beside Jubal Mann.

The boy – no more than fourteen – snapped, and his demented screams threatened to start panic so that an officer ended up shooting him. It took Jubal and Ruben a long time to recover from that incident, but over the next year they became hardened sol-diers, sometimes laughed about the dead arm panic, telling it often, making it into a macabre joke so as to improve their image as hard-bitten fighting men to new recruits who had come straight from the enlist-ment office to the battleground. Callously and deliberately they turned the newcomers' stomachs with vivid descriptions . . . a repeat of their own treat-ment when they had first enlisted.

They survived horrific battles, looked out for each other, were even wounded in the same fight and shared a hospital tent until they recovered.

Then, in the fifth year, came Murder Ridge – given that name after a terrible ten day bombardment by Yankee artillery; unceasing, high explosive and incendiary shells, raining out of the sky, day and night. Their troop was supposed to be relieved within twenty-four hours, but they ran out of food and ammunition, had to get their drinking water from puddles in the bottom of powder-smelling, corpse-fouled shellholes. . . .

Then, ten days after the bombardment began,

there was one final, terrible barrage, obviously intended to totally annihilate them. John Mundy was hurled around, a huge, searing blast slamming him into the ground with such force he marvelled his spine didn't break. When he regained consciousness, he found to his horror he was the only one still alive. He was wounded in the hip and shoulder on his left side but – *he was alive!*

Jubal had been horribly mutilated by a shell blast and the only way Mundy recognized his corpse was by the boots on legs that were almost severed from the rest of Jubal's body. Earlier, to wile away the time in the barrage, forced to cower like rats in their trenches and dug-outs, they had cut letters from a dead comrade's old leather belt – J,M,R,B – and sewn them on their boots: *J* and *M* on Jubal's; *R* and *B* on Mundy's. His left boot had had the heel shot off and his right was torn up by shrapnel. As he took the same size as Jubal he exchanged boots, thinking to himself as he pulled them on that he would likely have to explain the initials J and M to people who knew him as Ruben Beck. . . .

That was when the idea came to him: why not *be* Jubal Mann? *Jube* didn't have any enemies that Mundy knew of, he didn't have some crazy old man looking to kill him and he knew that Old Man Tomkin and Seth were still searching, even after all this time. They had been asking around for John Mundy only a couple of months back when the troops had been marching through the Big Cat River valley. Luckily he was wearing a dirt-clogged beard at the time, his ragged hair shoulder-long, and walked right past them, heart hammering as he glimpsed that crazy, hot-eyed old face. He passed without being recognized.

Now there was no one else left alive in the troop, he was confident he could pull off masquerading as Jubal Mann. He and Jubal had exchanged their life stories in intimate detail on many a night of dreary guard duty. He knew more than enough to pass for Jubal, unless he was unlucky enough to run into someone who knew him. . . .

But the Yankees put paid to any chance of that.

He awoke the morning after taking Jubal Mann's identity to find Yankee soldiers had moved on to the ridge that they had pounded to blood-soaked dust. They took him prisoner at bayonet point, an oddity, a lone survivor to be paraded for the amusement of the men in Union Blue who had blasted a hundred Rebels to oblivion. *He* was the only live Johnny Reb most of them had seen close-up since the war began; they called him 'Jube The Man', thought it was funny.

The prison camp was far from 'funny': it almost killed him, but, after a year, half-starved, beaten and reviled, he heard that the war was finally winding down.

And when the opportunity came, he escaped, not long before the South at last admitted defeat. He didn't even bother reporting back to his lines: total surrender was a foregone conclusion by then.

So he began building a peacetime life for himself – as Jubal Mann. . . .

'And I've been Jubal ever since,' he completed his story. 'He was a loner, too, never had anyone to call kin, so I figured I was pretty safe from being recognized as an impostor. I'm sorry I had to describe Jubal's death in such ugly terms, Andy, but I-I wanted you to understand that there was no possible chance that he might have survived. But I never expected anything like – this.'

She was still sitting on the edge of the bed, the gun was pointed at him, though she rested it on her thigh now. He saw the glisten of tears on the beautiful ivory face but she still had a look of determination about her; the set jaw, compressed lips.

'Why did Jubal think he had no living kin?' she asked huskily.

'You get to hear all kinds of things, recruits bringing news from all over the country, some credible, some simply made up in an effort to impress the old hands. I don't know the details – Jubal wouldn't talk about them – but he was mighty upset about the argument he'd had with his father over joining the army. He took off, as you'll know, and stubbornly went to war like he wanted to, but, later, someone told him about a family named Mann being massacred by Comanche renegades near the Staked Plains. He already knew about his father's wagon train being wiped out in the San Juan mountains. He was sure the family was his, had to be, he kept saying – just as he kept saying he should've been there to help, stayed home to fight for them instead of running off to war. It made no difference that he would have been slaughtered along with the others if he had – he just felt he'd deserted his family when they needed him.'

She nodded slowly. 'Yes – that would be Jubal. A strong sense of family. Both he and father were stubborn. They must've had a terrible row for Jubal to go like he did.'

'You were old enough to recall him?'

The redhead moved side to side, the silky hair briefly sweeping across her pale face. 'No – strangely enough I never really knew him. He'd left while I was less than a year old. But Ma never stopped talking about him, so I knew almost everything about him – including that he never had any kind of a birthmark – like that one on your chest.'

So that was what had given him away. . . .

Her voice trailed off and he pulled on a shirt. She still held the gun but it was no longer cocked and she didn't seem to realize she had it until he suddenly reached out and took it from her.

She gasped and jumped to her feet. 'Give me that!'

'You don't need it – I don't intend to harm you. In any case, shouldn't you be getting back to the theatre for your show?'

She looked at him coolly. 'My part doesn't start till after the interval, but I want my gun! It's saved my life at least once.'

He deftly spilled the two small-calibre cartridges

from the gun and handed it back to her. She curled one full red lip disdainfully at him. 'Thank you,' she said sulkily.

'Do you think you can – should – go on stage? After this upset. . . ? Which I apologize for.'

She almost smiled. 'Don't you know the theatre tradition – *the show must go on*?' She tried to make it light, but it sounded forced and he knew she had been badly shaken by his story.

'Well, if you feel up to it. Have you got time before you need to leave to tell me how *you* survived the massacre of your family. . . ? Jubal never knew you were alive or I'm sure he would've gone looking for you. Do you feel up to that?'

Her hazel eyes glistened and she dabbed at them quickly with a lace 'kerchief, sat down again on the edge of the bed. She hesitated, then shook her head, keeping her eyes lowered.

'No – no, I don't really – *I don't want to think about that awful time!*'

She was trembling now, wouldn't look at him. He heard her trying to stifle a sob, started to reach out to touch her forearm, but she suddenly stood, ran to the door and hurried from the room.

He lunged for the open door, but she was already halfway down the stairs and, feeling awkward, confused about how he should react, he stopped on the landing and watched her swiftly cross the foyer and go out on to the dark street.

Hurrying like the Devil himself was after her.

CHAPTER 6

'ANDY'

The 'show' did go on, but not for long.

Andrea collapsed, screaming briefly, in the middle of a scene during the Troupe's light-hearted version of *A Midsummer Night's Dream: Or, Was it More Than a Dream.* Oberon and Titania were in the early stages of 'affection' – the programme tactfully explained – while the impish Puck acted as voyeur, passing on his 'observations' to a curious and appreciative audience.

Andrea was cast as Queen of the Fairies, wearing diaphonous clothing that (by clever dressmaking and the careful placement of flesh-coloured material) seemed to reveal a lot more of her beautiful body than it actually did.

The collapse at first was considered to be part of the irreverent adaptation of The Bard's work, until the rowdy audience realized her scream had been more horrific than comic.

The curtains rushed down and there was much activity on stage behind them. The audience was on its feet, shouting, demanding to know what had happened. The actor playing the part of Puck poked his head through the joint in the curtains and announced with only a bare hint of the levity and sly lasciviousness that dominated his on-stage dialogue: 'We beseech thy patience, dear audience.' Then, voice reverting to normal, with real concern, added, 'Our leading lady, An-dray-uh, has suddenly become discombobulated.' Here he dropped his voice a little and said, with barely concealed scorn, 'That's "confused" to you peasants.' Then he raised his voice again, forcing a Puckish smile. 'A doctor is in attendance and we crave your indulgence for a few minutes longer while we move on to another part of our show.'

Catcalls, threats of demanding ticket money back, and then, in his best Puckish voice, the actor announced: 'Oooh, what do I here, addressing such a wonderful gathering of the woodfolk, when I could be assisting our physician in his labours, examining our fair Fairy Queen, removing her gossamer gowns and—' He gave the audience a straight face, flicked his eyebrows, hitched a hip and closed the curtains, with a final, gravelly, 'Yea! What the *hell* am I doing out here, wasting time with you lot?' He disappeared through the curtains. 'Fare thee well!'

He was a popular actor and got a laugh, but there was still plenty of furore. Pendleton and Truscott shrugged, the rancher saying to a tense Jubal, 'We'll wait, I think. These things happen occasionally and can't be helped. Are you all right, Jubal?'

Mann stood abruptly, looking at the stage curtains which were bulging and swaying with the movement of people behind them. 'I'm going to find out what's happened.'

'Sit down, friend. You can see what's happened, man!' the banker exclaimed. 'The woman fainted, had some kind of a fit, I imagine.' He smiled slightly. 'Or she may even be drunk. It's not unknown for these stage people to—'

'You don't know what you're talking about,' Jubal snapped, starting to make his way along the leg-tangled aisle between the seats. 'It was a genuine collapse!'

Truscott blinked and Pendleton stared as Jubal thrust people roughly aside and stormed down the aisle towards the stage. He wrenched the curtains open for a moment while he stepped through. Bryce Pendleton shook his head.

'He sounds genuinely upset.'

Truscott nodded curtly. 'He'll be back. They'll throw him out of there very smartly, I imagine.'

But the improvised scene was set up and the actors took their places and began their performance – yet there was still no sign of Jubal. . . .

Pendleton and Truscott settled back, puzzled, half their attention on the curtained part of the stage.

Andrea had been removed to her dressing room.

The doctor worked over her and some of the cast who weren't required for the show at that moment did their best to keep jostling gawkers away from the door. Jubal forced his way in, even drawing his Colt. The show peoples' eyes bulged as they backed up and the medic, grey-haired and crotchety, looked around. 'What the devil d'you think you're doing?'

Jubal stood over the medic who crouched beside the narrow bed where Andrea lay, still unconscious.

'Giving you some working room, Doc. She's my sister,' he said, stretching things a little. 'We haven't seen each other in over ten years and . . . I gave her some bad news about the family. Could it've caused this?'

'Very likely. Her pulse is erratic, which means her heart is beating irregularly. She's sweating profusely, yet her skin is cold to the touch – symptoms of shock. I may need to administer digitalis to settle her down. But there is always a certain amount of risk with that particular drug. . . .'

'How many times have you had it react badly, Doc?'

Reluctantly, the doctor said, 'Only once and that was more than enough! But she's young and fit. There's no real reason why she should have any problems.'

'If you don't give it to her?'

'Then, young man, she may well pass into a coma, and recovery will indeed be in the lap of the Gods, as they say.'

'Go ahead and give it, Doc. I accept responsibility.'

Relief softened the medic's wrinkled features and he opened his black bag, rummaging amongst the hexagonal dark brown bottles and set one on a small table. He brought out a conical glass graduated in fluid drams, carefully measured the dose, a few drops at a time.

'Put that damn gun away and lift her head so I can give it to her.'

Jubal did as he was asked. The girl, pale, despite her stage make-up, coughed but swallowed the full dose.

Jubal, anxious, asked, 'How long before you know if it's going to work?'

'Only a matter of minutes.' The sawbones sounded tense too, holding the girl's slim wrist, his lips moving as he counted the pulse beats. He frowned once, then relaxed and looked up with the beginnings of a smile. 'It's taking effect but she'll need to rest.' He glanced at some of the show people still crowding the narrow doorway. 'She can't appear on stage any more tonight – perhaps not for several nights.'

'Oh, dammit to hell!' snapped one of the men, who turned out to be the producer, director and male star of the skit all rolled into one. He glared wildly at the other actors. 'Do we have an understudy capable of taking Andy's place?'

Jubal unholstered his Colt and ushered them out as they settled into an animated discussion. As he did so, Deputy Link Barnes appeared, entered and confronted him.

'What's this about you pulling a gun on the saw-bones?' He stopped, dropping a hand to his own gun, but relaxed slightly when Jubal holstered his Colt. 'That's better.'

Obviously, someone had sent for him.

'It's all right, Deputy,' the doctor spoke up. 'It was a misunderstanding. This man is the young lady's brother and was anxious about her collapse. Nothing to worry about.'

Barnes glared at Jubal. 'You're *her* brother. . . ?'

Jubal nodded but the deputy still looked sceptical. 'Why all this trouble because she fainted?'

'A little more than that,' snapped the doctor, looking at Jubal. 'She had some bad news. I don't know what it was but it must've had a tremendous impact on her – it put her in a state of shock, blanked out her mind.'

'Sounds queer to me. What was the news that was so damn bad? You give it to her, Mann?'

Jubal nodded. 'It's none of your business, Barnes.'

The deputy straightened, jaw hardening. 'Now, s'pose I make it my business?'

'You can try.'

Both men dropped their hands to their gun butts but froze as a child's voice said suddenly,

'*Who was that man, Mumma?*'

All three looked sharply at Andrea. Her eyes were still closed, though they could see the eyeballs behind the lids flicking back and forth rapidly as if she was reading very quickly. Her lips moved and the small voice – that of 'Andy', the girl child who liked

81

to dress up and play at being a boy – spoke again:

'I don't like him, Ma. I'm glad he's going away and not staying for supper. Oh, please don't cry, Mumma! Our daddy's not dead! That old man in his dirty army jacket was telling lies! He must've been! My daddy's coming home. Oh, Mumma! You can't see through those glasses with tears in your eyes. Can I look. . . ? Oh, goody – he's way out on the plain now and it's growing dark and soon I won't be able to see him at all. . . .'

Suddenly, the piping voice took on a note of alarm, which swiftly changed to terror.

'*Mumma*! There – there's an Indian! He's talking to an – Indian! Oh, I'm scared, Mumma, I'm—' A sudden scream made the listeners jump. 'There's more Indians! An' – an' they're riding this way. . . !'

Jubal, Doctor Field, and Deputy Barnes all held their breath, watching the girl on the bed as she grimaced with returning memories she had probably blocked from her mind years ago. . . .

She thrashed about, hands screwing up the blanket that covered her, the doctor and Jubal holding her arms, feeling the surprising power in her as remembered terror took hold. Her eyes were wide open now, staring at some horror only she could see. . . .

Liza Mann pulled herself together and hurriedly closed the shutters, ordering the others to drop the bars into place. Melvin Mann was always saying he would be happier if the shutters and bars were of heavier timber, but he had never quite got around to replacing them.

Liza, still shaken by the captain's bad news about Mel's death, hurriedly got the few firearms they possessed. All were old, well-used cap-and-ball weapons that took a long time to reload. Even the young children knew how to pour a measure of powder into the chamber, drop in the ball, then a wad, and tamp it down, slip a percussion cap over the nipple so the gun was ready to fire. But it all took time.

The Indians seemed to know this; they made a wild, savage, attack with plenty of blood-curdling yells, shooting their trade rifles, hurling rocks against the shutters. Liza and her brood fired their weapons at the screaming, hard-riding painted men stretched out along their war ponies. One horse was hit and tumbled in a thrashing of dust and flailing legs, its rider hurtling off to one side. An Indian with a fire arrow fitted to his bow was hit too, but not before he had released his shaft and it quivered in the grass-covered roof of the soddy.

The dry grass blazed, practically exploding into flames. Shutters splintered. The children were crying, while they fumbled to re-load. Liza felt sick when she realized how she had fallen into the raiders' trap: the attack had been all-out to make them shoot off their weapons. In the lull while they were laboriously reloading they would sweep in again and. . . .

Only the Spencer was a repeater and she had few magazines of spare cartridges for that. But while the children whined and sobbed and fumbled, she fired through a splintered loophole, cried out involuntarily as an arrow quivered right beside the opening, a bare inch from her face. She got off her shot but wasn't sure if she hit the warrior or not.

Shaking as she tore out an empty magazine and pushed a loaded tube into the rifle butt, she turned to Frannie.

'Take the young ones to The Pit! *Now*! Don't cry protest, children! Go with Frannie. Macy and I can hold off these red devils, can't we Macy?'

The boy, white and strained looking, cocked the old Dragoon pistol his father had left for him, held it in both hands as he nodded and fired. The huge weapon was too heavy to jump much, but he felt the thudding recoil through his wrists and almost dropped it. Then he yelled and the shutter splintered as a tomahawk drove into the wood. Through the now jagged loophole he stared directly into the reddened, mad eyes of a Comanche warrior and jumped back, dropping the Dragoon in his fright at such a close encounter.

When he stooped to pick it up, the motion saved his life. A stone-headed lance thrust through and ripped his shirt. If he hadn't stooped, he would have been impaled.

By then Frannie had taken the young ones below by way of a hidden trapdoor to The Pit – a hole dug beneath the flooring with a partly completed tunnel angling off one corner towards the creek; another job Mel hadn't gotten around to completing, and now never would.

Liza started shooting again with the Spencer. Smoke was curling down now from the blazing roof. She and Macy coughed and wiped tears from their eyes. Frannie came back, picked up her old single-shot musket with the floppy trigger and suddenly screamed her mother's name, whirling and firing the weapon.

Liza jumped around as the heavy ball thrummed past her head, and was in time to see the painted face of a Indian explode in a red splash as he came through a window after he had kicked in the splintered shutter.

In moments, others had taken the dead man's place, more shutters were beaten in and the room filled with wild-eyed whooping Comanche, scalping knives and tomahawks already in their hands. . . .

Liza sobbed as Frannie collapsed, transfixed by an arrow through her slim young body, then, crying and asking the Good Lord's forgiveness, she used her last shot to kill Macy outright – these devils would never torture or scalp him alive. *She wished she had one more bullet – for herself. But her gun was empty and there was nothing she could do now as they closed in, reaching for her with blood-soaked hands. . . .*

The terrible screams as the butchery began penetrated the trapdoor and down into The Pit where Hal and Andy and Will cowered. Little Andy was almost too terrified to move and Will picked her up and thrust her way back into the dark hole the start of the escape tunnel that had been intended to eventually lead to the creek bank.

She fought and kicked, terrified out of her mind. Will slapped her hard enough to make her gasp and briefly bring her to her senses. 'Stay there!' he croaked.

Then the trapdoor was wrenched up and two Indians, bare legs clanking with bone and metal charms, streaked with fresh blood, jumped down among the terrified children, the light of the lone candle stub glinting off their already gory knives.

One had a shotgun and he fired it over the childrens' heads, laughing wildly at their cringing. The blast extinguished the candle and drowned out the hysterical screaming of the children. . . .

But it also tore loose an avalanche of dirt from the un-shored roof, filling The Pit with choking dust, and cutting off Andy from the others, plunging her into total stygian darkness, with neither sight nor sound as the cave-in filled the tunnel from floor to roof. . . .

Instantly came the onset of a new terror as she realized she was now buried alive.

CHAPTER 7

BREAKING NEWS

The headlines of the weekly Cheyenne *Clarion. Special Edition,* cried out in forty-eight point type:

Leading Lady Real-Life Heroine!
Exclusive by Ned Stewart

There was a grainy photograph of *An-dray-uh,* star of the touring stage show playing at the Cheyenne Rialto Theatre, with the first few paragraphs describing the story of the Staked Plains massacre. At the foot of page one were the words 'Continued on page three'.

The graphic descriptions leaped off the page to hit the reader right between the eyes.

'*The terrible gut-grasping fear wrenched pitiful cries from the Mann children, innocent babes of the prairie. . . .*

'*These same children, despite their overwhelming terror,*

fought valiantly against the blood-thirsty Red Demons from Hell. . . .'

And so it went on in the unrestrained yellow journalism of the day. And the *Clarion* was far from pro-Indian.

Jubal Mann first read it – or part of it – over his breakfast in the hotel and quickly lost his appetite. Pendleton had his own copy of the rag and he sat back with a gasp, looking steadily at Jubal's rock face.

'My God! Allowing for this Stewart's over-enthusiastic writing, this young lady – your sister, I believe? – has suffered terribly! No wonder she collapsed last night. Jubal? Where are you going? You haven't done more than nibble at your breakfast.'

By then the glass doors of the dining room were swinging closed behind Jubal Mann. He strode across the foyer, noticing the clerks and two other guests with their noses buried in the *Clarion.*

His hands were clenched into fists as he hurried along the boardwalk, cannoning into people, rudely thrusting them aside, no apologies. They stared belligerently after him, some men shouting. He ignored them all, crossed the street, disdaining the traffic of riders and spring wagons alike, once again ignoring the angry shouts directed at him and finally reached the gaily painted frame building of the Cheyenne *Clarion – First In Wyoming, First With The News.*

He straight-armed the doors open and crossed the small foyer to the startled receptionist. As she looked up into his taut face she felt glad there were several brass upright bars between her and this angry cowboy.

'S-Sir. . . ?'

'Ned Stewart.'

'I'm afraid Mr Stewart—'

'Mr Stewart's the one who should be afraid. Come on, lady! Where'll I find him! Pronto, now!'

Frightened, the woman swallowed and pointed a trembling finger through the bars at a half-glass door with the words *Chief Editor* painted on them.

'B-but I don't think they should be disturbed. . . .'

Her voice trailed off as Mann reached the door and opened it so roughly that it slammed back against the wall and a great lightning streak of a crack whipped from corner to corner of the glass panel.

Two men were in the office; a lean one in shirt sleeves with elastic armbands, lounging in a chair with long legs straight out, a half-smoked cigar on its way to his thin-lipped mouth. Across the desk another man sat; older, plumper, wearing a silk vest with a gold watch chain looped across his ample middle, and a twin to the other cigar jammed in a corner of his rubbery mouth. He started to rise in indignation. 'What in thunder are you. . . ?'

Mann ignored him, lunged at the startled man with the armbands, slapped the cigar from his hand, bunched up the striped shirtfront and yanked him bodily out of the chair. He was shorter than Jubal but was held on his tiptoes so he could look into Mann's blazing eyes.

'Your name Stewart?' The man, blinking, mouth slack, nodded. 'You wrote that article about Andrea?

Dammit, *An-dray-uh*?' He shook the man so roughly his reply was unintelligible, but Stewart nodded vigorously. Mann threw him across the room, overturning the chair, the journalist sliding into the wall with a crash.

By then the plump editor was on his feet, reaching hurriedly into a desk drawer which he wrenched open. Jubal saw him and whipped out his Colt, thumb on the hammer spur. The editor jumped back, lifting both hands to show they were empty.

'Jesus Christ, man! Wh-what do you want?'

'I'll get to you in a minute.' Jubal dragged the dazed Stewart to his feet and rammed the muzzle of the six-gun under the quivering jaw. 'Open up! *Open* damn you!'

Stewart fearfully opened his mouth and sucked in a sharp breath as the barrel slid between his lips, the blade foresight cutting the roof of his mouth, drawing blood.

'You son of a bitch! Basically that article's true but you've made it into a horror story that'll give half the kids in Wyoming nightmares for weeks! *Where did you get it? Who – told – you?*' He shook the man violently.

The editor spoke but his voice was shaky. 'A newspaperman is not required to diviuge the source of his information, mister. That's the unwritten law of journalism – and, speaking of law—'

'Don't!' snapped Mann without turning, looking into the bulging eyes of Ned Stewart. He cocked the hammer back fully with a click that made Stewart's legs turn to water. 'You're about to break that stupid "law", Stewart, or your fat slug of a boss is going to be washing your brains off the wallpaper! Which'll it be?'

But he was talking to an unconscious man. Stewart's weight dragged at Jubal's arm and he let him fall with a clatter, swinging the gun towards the editor. 'Want to join him?'

The editor swallowed, obviously considering Mann to be insane. Well, his life was more important to him than being stubborn over something that actually had no legal standing at this point in time, he decided.

'I-I believe Ned was approached by Deputy Barnes,' the editor gasped. 'We – we paid him $250 for the story. He swore he was a witness to the girl telling it after her collapse.'

Jubal nodded slowly. 'The son of a bitch was there all right. Know where I'll find him right now?'

The editor started to shake his head, then said hurriedly, 'I believe he was celebrating his windfall last night in the Straight Eight saloon. It stays open twenty-four hours a day. In fact we've been campaigning against it for—'

The editor sagged into his chair as Jubal stormed out, slamming the door after him for good measure. The jar completed the destruction of the glass panel. As the shards fell musically, the editor winced and noticed that Stewart had wet his pants.

In a choked voice he called: 'Someone fetch the sheriff!'

Before he reached the bright red batwings of the Straight Eight, Jubal saw Doctor Field hurrying towards him, clutching a crumpled newspaper. He knew it could only be a copy of the *Clarion*.

The medic took one look at Jubal's face and stopped. 'I gather you've read this abominable article.'

'Just seen Ned Stewart about it,' Jubal gritted.

Field said quickly, 'I hope you don't think I had anything to do with giving him Andrea's story.'

'No, Doc. It was Link Barnes.'

'Damn that man! Jubal, I have a young trainee nurse who works the early morning shift and, look, she doesn't know any better, thought it would cheer Andrea up, seeing her name in the paper.'

'Christ! She showed it to Andy?'

'I'm afraid so. There was some . . . hysteria. I-I've had to sedate her. She'll probably be all right, but it's a real setback to her recovery.'

Jubal spun on his heel and stomped up on to the walk, slamming through the batwings.

The smoke-hazed barroom was surprisingly busy for this time of day, most of the customers red-eyed, some sleeping at the drink-stained tables, indicating they had been here for quite some time, probably all night.

Link Barnes was at the bar, glanced into the ornate mirror behind it and spun quickly when he saw Jubal striding down towards him. He thrust up, swaying some from all the booze he had put away during his 'celebration'.

'What's your trouble, Mann?' he said, his words a little slurred. 'I'm warnin' you – don't start anythin' you can't finish.'

He almost climbed on the bar as he realized Jubal wasn't going to stop. He came right up to Barnes, straightarmed the deputy hard enough to bend him back across the counter. He grabbed the man's trouser belt and hauled him forward, slapping an open hand back and forth rapidly across the startled deputy's stubbled face.

Chairs tipped over as men jumped hurriedly to their feet. The barkeep looked uncertain about just what he should do as blood splashed across the mirror when it spurted from Barnes's nose.

Jubal hauled Barnes forward and threw him bodily into the nearest set of tables and chairs. Men there hurriedly scattered as the deputy rolled to the floor, fending off the table as it fell across him. He kicked wildly to get to his feet and immediately reached for his six-gun. Jubal's was already in his hand and he smashed it down across the deputy's wrist. Bone cracked and Link Barnes yelled, snatching the injured arm across his chest as his gun fell to the floor. Jubal stepped forward, thrust his dead-white face within inches of Barnes's contorted features and gritted, 'If she doesn't recover, I'll come back and finish this, you gabby bastard!'

The gun barrel struck twice, once swinging backhanded and splitting Barnes's cheek open, and again coming back and mashing his lips and two of his teeth. He gagged, staggered, legs buckling. He fell to his knees, hand cupped under his ruined face, catching blood. Jubal lifted a foot into his chest and thrust, stretching him out on the floor. His head rapped hard against the brass foot rail.

There was silence in the saloon except for Barnes's wet, stertorous breathing. Jubal looked around, saw that no one was going to take up the unpopular deputy's fight for him, and holstered his Colt. He slapped a five dollar coin on to the counter.

'Have a drink on me,' he told the barkeep and turned and moved stiffly towards the batwings.

Before he reached them, they slapped open and Sheriff Gower stood there with a sawed-off shotgun.

He glanced at the bloody, unconscious deputy, his face expressionless. 'Someone get the sawbones.'

Two men hurried out, looking as if they were glad to be leaving.

'Think you and me'd better have a talk, Mann.' Gower jerked his head, the shotgun covering Jubal. 'Come on down to the office – unless you want to argue about it?'

Jubal shook his head. 'I'm with you, Sheriff. Just don't get an itch in that trigger finger.'

'Let's go.'

In the law office, Gower sat down at his desk and gestured with the shotgun for Mann to take the chair opposite. He laid the gun down next to his right hand on the desktop.

'Tell me.'

Jubal told it succinctly and Gower reached down

and picked up a rolled copy of the *Clarion*. Obviously he hadn't yet opened it. But he did so now and glanced at the front page, turned to page three and looked up.

'Kid's had a rough time of it. You, too, I guesss. How'd you feel about being away when it happened?'

'How d'you think I felt,' Jubal said, wary now.

'That's what I'm askin' you.'

'It – didn't set well,' he said slowly, remembering the real Jubal's reaction when he learned a family named 'Mann' had been massacred on the Staked Plains. 'Wished I'd stuck around instead of actin' like a fool and runnin' off to go to war.'

'Typical young feller's reaction, the juices of youth and so on. The army must've looked a lot better than boring days tryin' to scratch a livin' in that graveyard country.'

Mann was surprised at Gower's understanding of young Jubal's actions. Then, obviously temporarily reminiscent: 'Had a son younger'n you did the same thing. Fell at Wilson's Field, three weeks later. . . .' He shifted in his chair. 'Still, if you'd stayed, you'd've been killed, too.'

Jubal nodded, believing it safer not to reply.

'Well, you didn't, and now there's the problem of your sister.' Gower's face suddenly hardened, steely eyes nailing Jubal. 'You beat the hell out of a duly-sworn deputy of my town, Mann—'

'He was there when Andy – Andrea – told it. He went straight to Ned Stewart and sold her story for $250.'

95

Gower continued to stare at him coldly. Then he sat back. 'Always was a mercenary sonuver, our Link.'

'Doc Field's young nurse showed the paper to Andy, thought she'd be happy to see her name in print, like most folk would be. Gave her hysterics. Doc said it's set back her recovery quite a deal.'

Gower's lips tightened. 'That goddamned Barnes! One of these men who blunder through life, causin' all kindsa trouble, standin' in the middle, untouched.' He drummed his fingers against the shotgun and Jubal tensed. The eyes flicked up to meet Jubal's again. 'Son of a bitch deserved all he got. Now, you never heard me say that, and you won't get much chance to slip up and say I did, 'cause you're leavin' town. And this time you ain't comin' back – savvy?'

Jubal released a breath he hadn't realized he had been holding. He shook his head and gave the sober lawman a half-smile. 'Whatever you say, Sheriff. I'm obliged, but—'

'No "buts"!'

'Just one, Sheriff – I've got to see Andy before I go. I have to know she's gonna be OK. You let me do that and I'll go without any trouble.'

'Which is how you'll go anyway. All right. Go see Doc Field and once you're sure your sister's gonna be OK, you hit the trail. Now, I'm gonna take a chair out on to the porch and I'm gonna smoke a pipe or two, and I'll be watchin' for you ridin' past, might even give you a farewell wave. Exactly one hour from now, that's your deadline and you stick to it or you ain't gonna be leavin' for a looooong time. I reckon Ned Stewart and Nichols, the chief editor, will be here right soon, too, wanting to know what I'm gonna do about you.'

Jubal stood, nodded curtly and started for the door.

He paused as Gower said, 'Unless . . . you want a deputy's job?' But he added quickly, shaking his head at some unspoken question he had asked himself, 'Nah, forget it – you'd gimme more ulcers than I've already got. On your way.'

'*Muchas gracias*, Sheriff. *Adios.*'

Jubal hurried out, not believing his luck: Luke Gower, one of the toughest lawmen ever to fork a saddle and trigger a shotgun, showing leniency! *To him!*

Well, Jubal was never one to look the proverbial gift horse in the mouth. He rubbed his sore knuckles, stepped down from the porch and hurried towards Doc Field's infirmary.

CHAPTER 8

AFTERMATH

Doc Field was straightening up from tending someone in a bed down at the end of the narrow room when Mann entered. As the medic turned, Jubal saw the patient was Link Barnes.

He seemed to be unconscious or just sleeping, heavy bandages across his nose, puffed and mashed lips smeared with salve. His breathing was slow and heavy, snorted through crushed nostrils.

'He's going to need a good deal of dental work.' The sawbones was tight-lipped and his eyes were not friendly. 'As well as packing of that nose and he has mild concussion.'

'He's the one sold Andy's story, Doc.' Jubal spoke off-handedly, looking towards Andrea's bed which he had almost reached. 'He ain't my worry.'

'No, I just don't like to see any human being battered and maimed, Jubal. Oh, I understand your feelings, and perhaps I would feel the same way if she was my sister, but—' He paused, shaking his head. 'I never had you picked for such callousness. That was very brutal.'

'Forget it, Doc – I wish I'd killed him. Anyway, never mind Barnes, how about Andy?'

'She's still sleeping as you can see.'

'Yeah, I can see that much, Doc,' Jubal replied shortly. 'That's the short-term, how about the long term?'

The medic heaved a deep breath, obviously calming his outrage. 'I believe she'll be all right. It's my opinion she's blocked out her horror of that massacre all these years. Your sudden appearance brought it all back with a rush and, well, she simply couldn't handle it. And, as is usual with the human body, when things reach that stage, it just closed down. In Andrea's case, she collapsed.'

'Yeah, but how's she gonna be when she wakes up? I mean, seein' that damn horror story that Stewart made out of it couldn't've done her a lot of good.'

'Not at all, I'm sorry to say, but she's got plenty of inner strength and I think now, with proper rest, she'll come good and get over it.' He looked sharply at Jubal. 'Especially if she realizes she's no longer alone in the world, family-wise.'

Jubal tensed, frowning. 'What're you saying, Doc?'

'I think you know. She'll stand a much better chance of recovery if you're with her.'

'But – I'm not really her brother. I told you, I only took his name!'

'Then you also should take some of his responsibilities.'

Jubal moved uncomfortably. 'Judas, Doc, I-I dunno. I want to help but— Look, she knows I'm not her real kin.'

'But you had years with her brother that she was denied. You know more about him than she does; she identifies you with the real Jubal. You were honest with her about taking his identity. Admittedly, it was a shock, but when she recovers, she'll see that, based on that alone, you can be trusted. It will make all the difference, Jubal, believe me.'

'Well, it's just not gonna be, Doc. Gower's given me an hour to get out of town and not come back. I've got Pendleton to think about, too, and this deal we've made.'

'Bryce Pendleton is a good man, Jubal. He'll understand.'

'Goddammit, Doc! Are you suggesting I take her with me back to Texas?'

Field was shaking his head before Mann finished speaking. 'Good Lord, no. She needs *rest* and trailing all the way south wouldn't give her that.'

'Then what?'

'Calm down. I have a son who, at one time, intended to claim open range in the Tall Men and work it – you know that's a range of mountains northwest of Cheyenne?' Jubal nodded impatiently. 'Unfortunately, working alone after he built his cabin, he felled a tree but it dropped the wrong way, crushed both his lower legs. He was suffering for three days before he was found.' He paused to clear his was throat, this was obviously a sensitive subject with him. 'I had to amputate his lower right leg. Of course he had to abandon all thought of ranching: he's an accountant now, and a good one, uses crutches to get around.'

'Hell, I'm sorry, Doc.'

Field held up a hand. 'He's come to terms with it and so have his mother and myself – mostly. But what I'm telling you is that his cabin still stands. No doubt it needs some attention but Larry's a good craftsmen and it's well built, in the wilderness, lots of natural beauty and quiet. An ideal place for Andrea to spend her recovery time.'

Jubal frowned, digesting this. He sat down on the edge of an empty bed, took out tobacco and papers and rolled a cigarette. Doc held a match for him and their gazes met as Jubal dipped the end of his cigarette into the flame.

'I-I'm no nursemaid, Doc.' He swiftly held up a hand as the medic started to speak. 'But I owe something to Jubal, not just for using his name, but because of the friendship we had. We looked out for each other during the fighting and while there was nothin' dramatic, like saving each other's life, we did fight our way outta some tight spots, side by side.'

'I knew I could depend on you, Jubal.'

'Don't get too excited – Andy might not want to be alone with me in the wilderness, you know. It all comes down to her in the end.'

Soberly, Doc Field nodded. 'You're right, and that

just goes to show you do understand her situation. I don't think I could've chosen a better man for the job.'

Jubal grunted, glanced at the end bed where Link Barnes started to move around to a more comfortable position, grunting and snorting a couple of times, eyes closed.

'Well, it'll keep Gower outta my hair, if nothing else. But there might still be some trouble from Ned Stewart and that fat editor.'

'My brother-in-law happens to be one of the leading lawyers in Cheyenne – I'll have a word with him. At the very least, I'm sure he can stall off any legal action the *Clarion* might contemplate and he's smart enough to hit back with a counter-action that will have them running for cover.'

Jubal smiled crookedly, glanced down at the pale, sleeping Andrea and exhaled a plume of tobacco smoke.

'Yeah,' he breathed. 'I reckon she's gonna be all right, Doc, once we get to this cabin. But I'm gonna need more than the hour Gower's given me to get ready and I'll have to hit Pendleton or Truscott for a loan to buy the supplies and hire a couple of pack horses.'

'Well, why're you standing here talking about these things? Go and see Gower. Tell him I'll back your request for more time.'

Field spoke with a half-smile and Jubal nodded, flicked a brief, two-fingered salute from the brim of his hat and hurried out to make arrangements.

From the end bed, Link Barnes watched out of slitted, bruised eyes, malevolence tightening his battered face enough to make him gasp with the pain.

Bryce Pendleton was more than understanding.

'Yes, that poor young woman has gone through a lot and I agree with Doctor Field that she should rest and recover where there's peace and quiet. You tell the livery man and storekeeper what you need, Jubal, and to send the bills to me. You can pay me back when our breeding deal is in full swing and we're growing richer by the day.'

'That's mighty white of you, Bryce.'

Pendleton waved it aside casually and Jubal could see that the gesture wasn't just show: the man really wanted to help. Jubal felt he had chosen a fine partner for the breeding programme. They shook hands.

'I think I know where Doc's son's cabin is. If it's the one I'm thinking of, it's substantial notched logs and a riverstone fireplace, though the chimney is only shaped out of roofing iron. It's not all that far from my spread. If you get into any difficulties, bring Andrea down, or give a message to one of my outriders if they're about. Sometimes they spend a night in the cabin if the weather is bad.'

Jubal felt better about that. He didn't say anything to Doc or Gower or Pendleton, but he felt pretty nervous about the upcoming chore of being what he saw as a glorified nursemaid to Andy. Yet he was keen to do it, help her in any way he could. *He figured he at least owed her that much.*

Gower had been reluctant to extend the deadline but Doctor Field talked him round. The medic's brother-in-law, Counsellor Guy Breen, had stalled the assault case the *Clarion* was threatening to bring against Jubal but only because the massacre story had been syndicated and picked up by a string of papers with offices in New York.

The whole country would know of Andrea's ordeal – and the violent reaction of her brother – as the editor saw to it that *that* part was included as an end-piece to the main story. It never hurt to let the public know that a newspaperman's life was not as easy or as glamorous as the majority believed. . . .

As for Andy herself, she woke from her sedated sleep and Field gave her time to reorient herself before he tactfully told her of his plan for her to recuperate in the mountain cabin.

She was silent for a long time, her pale face composed, and then she raised her eyes to him and smiled faintly. 'You're very kind, Doctor. Jubal – I have to think of him that way! – can tell me lots of things I want to know about my brother. It's—' She put a hand to her forehead, blinking hard. 'I feel a little – overwhelmed – not sure I can take it all in.'

'Don't force it, my dear – Jubal has a lot to tell you. Just enjoy the mountain air and the wilderness. I don't know if you like wildlife, but there is a good deal of it up there . . . not all antagonistic to humans.'

Her face brightened. 'Good! I do like animals but

travelling with the show doesn't give me much time to enjoy a pet of my own – we're never in one place long enough.' She suddenly gasped and put a hand to her mouth. 'My stars! The show! I-I've forgotten about it!'

'Your manager has been here while you were sedated. He's confident your understudy will be able to take your place for a time. . . . Oh, I see by your face I've made a gaff, have I?'

She smiled slowly. 'Well, no leading lady likes to see her role taken from her, but Milly-Jane is quite good. Oh, that sounds condescending! I didn't mean it that way. She's new to the stage and really enjoys it. I'm glad she's going to get a break, because she has worked hard, and she walks better than I do, just seems to float across the stage – like a Fairy Queen should, I suppose.' Then she put on a mock severe face. 'But if you ever tell anyone I said so. . . .'

Doc Field chuckled. 'I get your point. Now, we'll run through the medicines I want you to take. It's not critical, but I would like you to follow my recommendations until you're really feeling better.'

Soberly she nodded. 'You're very thoughtful and obliging, Doctor. I didn't realize that bottling up those terrible memories could affect me so . . . prodigiously. I'm truly grateful.'

'Jubal is the one you should be thanking – I'm sure he's the real key to your recovery.'

A small frown appeared between her eyes. She nodded slowly and spoke almost to herself.

'Yes – I believe so, too.'

*

A week after the massacre article appeared in the Cheyenne *Clarion,* the Santa Fe *Gazette* ran the story as a double-page feature in the centre of the special eight-page edition.

Yet another frontier newspaper not noted for any sympathetic feelings towards Indians, there were several illustrations by a prominent Western artist of the day. Famous for 'action' in his drawings, these depicted screaming redmen astride truly magnificent war ponies, shooting arrows and repeating rifles into a diminutive sod hut in the middle of a vast, empty plain. Two female bodies were depicted impaled on several arrows; another showed an Indian standing with a foot on a child's body, holding aloft a dripping scalp. An older woman in a window of the hut held a Civil War musket to her shoulder, shooting at a menacing Indian with inky blood spurting from a chest wound. Another warrior rose behind him, with a blood dripping hatchet.

The presentation was about par for the course in the 1870s. People who lived in the safety of large towns apparently liked to see such horrors depicted in pen and ink, which was as close as they wanted to get to the reality.

And in a black-bordered frame below the end of the article was the *Clarion*'s indignant report about the 'unprovoked' attack on journalist Ned Stewart and chief editor Nicolls by the older brother of the small girl survivor. . . .

They named him in heavy typeface: Jubal Mann.

CHAPTER 9

THE WRITTEN WORD

The old Mexican woman swept the porch listlessly. It wasn't large – about seven feet by six – and was tagged on to the front of the small shingle-roofed ranch house.

Dust rose as she moved the broom and when she waved some aside so she could see, the rider coming in from the Albuquerque trail was visible. The mottled grey gelding told her who it was; Harrison Gale's wide shoulders and that hat that looked like it had been kicked from one end of the Manzano Ranges to the other clinched it. She had never seen any hat so shapeless and individual.

She began to mutter, scraping up a small pile of dirt and dead leaves from the apple trees. When Gale dismounted with a grunt and took a folded newspaper from one of his saddle-bags, she waited until he

107

turned and had his foot on the bottom step, then she swept the pile of dirt with a flourish and Gale jumped back as grit and twigs and leaves hit his chest, a few reaching his lower face.

'Goddamn you, you stupid greaser hag!' Gale snapped, whipping off his hat and slapping at his clothing, spitting to his left. 'You done that a'purpose.'

She looked wide-eyed, surprised – an expression she had worked on for a long time for just such occasions as this. She got just enough contriteness in her quavery voice.

'Ah, Señor Gale! *Arrepentido*! Sorry, *señor* – I was saying a prayer for Señor Stone and I had my eyes closed. Here, I will brush your clothes.'

'Get the hell away from me!' growled Gale stomping up on to the porch. 'I really thought you done it a'purpose I'd wring your scrawny neck.'

She put a hand to her saggy throat and widened her eyes even more. Gale smiled thinly, glad he had scared the old bitch.

'How is he today?'

The woman shook her head slowly and sadly. '*Muy malo*. The cough is bad and he feels – *triste*.'

'Hell, you'd be unhappy, too, if you had an Injun stone arrerhead floatin' around in your chest, a quarter inch from your heart.' He slapped the newspaper into his free hand and she jumped at the sound. 'I got somethin' here that'll make him feel *bueno* – *muy bueno*!'

He even tipped her a wink as he went into the

house and right through to the *ramada* at the rear
where Captain Gabriel Stone sat hunched in a rick-
etty-looking wheelchair, a blood-spotted kerchief
held against his mouth. His thin shoulders shook as
the cough that was killing him racked his frail body.

He was literally only a shadow of the man who, all
those years ago, ordered the massacre of the Mann
family in their soddy on the Staked Plains.

'You best give up smokin',' Gale said facetiously as
he sat down in a woven-grass chair beside the old
man. Actually, Stone was only in his late fifties but
looked over seventy.

He finished coughing and turned his gaze to Gale.
The cowboy found himself tensing, felt a queer knot
of fear in his mid-section: ailing or not, this old
bastard still had the power to turn a man's guts to
water when he really tried.

'You – you'll never – make a medicine – show
comedian, Gale. If I could lift a six-gun I'd – make –
damn sure of – that – right now.'

The emotion left him gasping and moments later
he was coughing again. Gale looked away as he spat
into the kerchief.

'Sorry, Skipper, mouth runs off sometimes before
I can stop myself.'

Stone glared. 'Work on it.'

Gale moved uncomfortably, unrolled the newspaper – a copy of the Santa Fe *Gazette*, already a week
old. He opened it in the middle and held the centre
spread for Stone to see.

'You readin' OK today?'

'Hold it closer,' rasped Stone, squinting.

Then the words must have come into focus for he straightened in the wheelchair, something Gale hadn't seen him do for weeks. He snatched the paper from Gale and it trembled in his grip.

The bitter, scaled lips moved as he read the words, stared at the graphic illustrations. Gale stayed silent, watching closely. He bet the old sonuver's heart was pounding. *Hell! He never thought! The shock might take him off. . . !*

He started to reach for the paper but the old man yanked it in close, chest heaving, and went on reading. Gale had time to roll and smoke a cigarette before he was through. Then Stone sat back in his chair hard enough to move it a few inches on its narrrow wire-spoked wheels in the sandy soil.

'You see that bit in the frame at the very bottom?'

After a fit of coughing, Stone lifted the paper and squinted as he read. He made a sound that scared Gale white: a kind of choking, whining, half-warcry sound in the back of his throat. The wrinkled face coloured deeply and he started to rise but was too weak and slumped back in his chair.

'Christ, Skipper. You want anythin'? Medicine? Whiskey. . . ?'

'Whiskey.'

Gale hurried back into the house and brought out a bottle and two glasses. Hell, *he* needed a whiskey almost as bad as the other! He hadn't expected this much reaction.

Gale handed Stone a drink, slopped some into a

glass for himself and lifted it high. 'Here's to livin' !' he said thoughtlessly in the working cowboy's traditional toast before cutting loose on payday to paint the town red.

'Oh, hell! I-I din' mean that. I mean, I—'

'Drink up and shut up!' snapped Stone in a surprisingly strong voice. He threw down his own drink and held the glass out for a refill. He downed half of that and sat hunched over, breath wheezing in the bony chest.

'So! Not only did Jubal Mann not die in the war, but there's still another goddam Mann alive that shouldn't be: the blond kid you told me was buried alive in that escape tunnel old Mel never finished diggin'.'

'Well—' Gale licked his lips, looked at the bottle and his empty glass, but something warned him not to take time to pour himself another drink right now. 'Half the roof had collapsed when one of them Injuns cut loose with his shotgun; the other kids were there, wailing an' screamin', an' one of 'em said "Andy" had been buried alive.'

'Jubal I can accept – we only had the army's word he was killed at Murder Ridge when the whole company was wiped out, but we had to take it.'

'Too many bits of bodies to be sure, I guess.'

Stone glared. 'I thought when I found out he was still alive, I'd taken care of him with the bounty – figured him for the last one – but now there's another one we didn't know about! Another Mann still livin' after I swore I'd wipe every last one of 'em,

111

every drop of Mann blood, off the face of the earth.'

Before he could stop himself, Gale said with a half grin, 'Yeah – the last Mann is a woman! Kinda funny, huh. . . ?' He quailed at the look on Stone's face.

'See how funny you think it is when you ride up to Cheyenne and send me a wire to say you've killed her! *Her!* Damn! Another surprise – Mel's woman called the kid Andy an' he – she – was wearin' boys' clothes. Ah! You get an outfit together and go *finish the job*! Don't you show your nose around here again until Jubal and this *An-dray-uh* are dead and buried. Take Wichita with you. It's time he started earnin' his keep.'

'Hell, Skipper, I got that widder-woman in Albuquerque all set for—' Gale stopped abruptly and stood up, nodding quickly as he saw Stone's face. 'Yeah, sure – me and Wichita – we'll be on the trail by sunup, Skip.'

'No you won't – you'll be on the trail by sun*down. Now get movin'.*'

He sagged back in the wheelchair, skin grey, breaths coming in rasping, wet-sounding gasps, one hand dangling over the side limply.

As Gale moved out, muttering under his breath, he paused and asked, 'We get the bounty when we nail him? Or you gonna put another one on the gall. . . ?'

'Get't . . . out!'

Gale got.

The sundown was gloriously coloured and fiery as

usual in the Manzanos. Golds and reds with streaks of luminous blue, steel-grey rolling clouds gilt-edged, the craggy mountains silhouetted like cardboard cutouts.

Shadows were heavy on the land as the sun was behind the range now. The blazing light slanted up dramatically and out there, heading north, were two riders, each leading a laden packhorse.

Captain Stone had refused to come indoors that evening at his usual hour. He wanted to see Gale and that gunfighter, Wichita, on their way. He had even tried to call out a farewell but he didn't have the breath and it only made him cough up more blood than usual.

But he felt good! Better than he had in a coon's age. He had been afraid he would die before someone nailed Jubal, but now he knew where the man was for sure and the new target, that damn girl, as well.

Two more Manns about to die.

Then he would die, too – die happy.

It was good to have something to hate again, even if only for a short time: it refreshed him. And this time he had high hopes of early news that there were no more Manns living on this earth.

He would have squared with Mel Mann after all this time. He just hoped the bastard was somewhere he could get to know that his whole damn family had been annihilated.

As his had been. . . .

'*Señor*, you have some of my enchilada soup for your supper? Or just a broth, if that is all you feel like.'

Stone cranked his head around slowly on his scrawny neck and the Mexican woman's mouth sagged as he rasped,

'Let's have some soup, Angelina, and some burritos, with *frijoles.* I've got me an appetite this night!'

'*Sí, señor,*' she said and as she turned away, and hurriedly crossed herself.

Madre de Dios! Señor Stone was actually smiling!

They were both surprised at how easy and comfortable they felt in each other's company.

Jubal tried to figure it out but reached no definite conclusion. Maybe it was because he knew so much about the real Jubal Mann and Andrea – Andy as she preferred to be called, now she was away from the stage – was hungry to know as much about her dead brother as possible.

One thing: he was relieved that she didn't hold it against him for taking her brother's name.

'What else could you do?' she answered when he asked if she felt he had done wrong. 'You had men who wanted to kill you still looking for you. Jubal – Jubal was past caring and seeing as you had been such good friends, I'm sure he would have approved.'

'He missed his family, Andy,' he told her quietly. 'He never really came to terms with running out on Mel – that's how he saw it. . . . He said he knew your father was a hard worker, a trier, but one of those men who seldom made the grade or reached the targets they had set themselves, no matter how hard they tried.'

She was sober and silent for a time, digesting his words. 'I was too young to know, but with hindsight, as I grew up I had a picture of my father working the longest hours, not just trying to make a living in that hard country but *fighting* it. Almost like a private war: he would beat the land, he would *win*, and I think when he realized he wasn't going to win, at least not as he really wanted, he grabbed the chance to lead that wagon train and get away from the drudgery of building the kind of ranch he had dreamed about.'

Jubal nodded slowly. 'Yeah, that way it wasn't really quitting.'

Her eyes were steady as she said, 'My father was not a quitter!'

'No, he wouldn't've taken on that wagon train chore if he was. Leading a hundred emigrants to Utah, with the war still going on, although winding down, was no easy thing.'

They were both silent then and he said slowly, 'I don't aim to upset you, Andy, but you seem quite at ease talking about your folks and the place in Texas right now so I was wondering – how did you get out of the tunnel? He sensed her tension. 'You *did* get out, that's what counts. If you find it hard to talk about. . . .'

'I dug my way out,' she told him, a mite tersely. 'There was a broken spade in the section where I was . . . entombed.' She shuddered. 'After all these years I can still bring back the terror I felt.'

They were sitting on a log in the mountain

115

evening, drinking coffee. A small camp-fire smouldered, the smoke helping keep the insects away. She had her hands clasped in her lap around her mug and in the dull light he could see how white her knuckles were.

'Strange, I actually remembered Pa breaking the handle on that spade.' She spoke slowly, without a lot of expression, looking off into the mountain shadows, perhaps hearing the night calls of the birds returning home to their roosts, the cough of a big cat drinking, buzz of mosquitoes, the stomp of the horses in the corrals behind the cabin. She didn't really seem aware of Jubal beside her.

'Pa never seemed to have enough time to do all the things he wanted. He would run from one job to the next, sometimes leaving one only half-finished, just following his impulses. He prepared The Pit so we could use it, but left it to dig a second well; then, before he'd finished that he was off felling lodgepole for corrals, then back to the escape tunnel that was to emerge on the creek bank where bushes would screen it. He worked almost frantically, and when the spade handle snapped, he threw it down and stomped away. He never got around to making a new handle.'

'Lucky for you, or the old spade might not have been left there.' She looked at him and then smiled slowly.

'Yes – of course.'

'Digging must've been one helluva job. How old were you? Only five?'

'Going on six. Yes, it was hard but the dirt was loose from the cave-in and I had some good luck.'

'Sounds as if you needed it.'

'Yes. I was only little, of course, and it was hard to breathe. The spade got heavy and I accidentally started some more loose dirt falling.'

'Hell!'

'No, it was my piece of good luck. Several pounds fell and buried me almost to my armpits. But then I saw some light. It was still night, of course, but my luck was in because the light was coming from the moon. It was in just the right position in the sky for me to see it.'

'How could you see it from underground?'

She smiled. 'Would you believe because I had broken into part of a rabbit warren? There are jackrabbits everywhere there. Macy used to hunt them and we ate plenty of them. Well, I'd broken through into one of the rabbit's tunnels. It certainly wasn't large enough for me to crawl through, but it was dry and crumbly and the spade broke large chunks out, which I had to work past my body. But it was only a few feet to the surface and I got out with some scratches and a lot of dirt in my hair.'

'Like you say, your piece of good luck.'

'Yes. The raiders had long gone and there was light in the east. I knew the Halstead place was east of ours so I started walking. It was well into the afternoon when Mr Halstead saw me staggering around. He took me home and he and his wife decided they were going to quit after the raid on our place. They took me with them and we went to Amarillo where some nuns took care of me.' She shrugged. 'I went to schools, and the nuns took me with them from town to town and . . . I grew up. A Sister Maria thought I could act a little and put me in concerts and so on and eventually I left and found work that led me to the travelling troupe.'

He regarded her soberly. She spoke matter-of-factly, wasn't looking for sympathy, simply stating what had happened.

'You've had it rough.'

'Oh, I don't know. Some of it was – the attack on the house and losing the entire family – but people were mostly kind to me. Sister Maria arranged acting lessons and, well, I got what I wanted – some education, a job I don't regard as work, but more of a pleasurable pastime. Not many people can say that.'

'Not many people could handle it the way you have, either.'

She looked down at the dying fire. 'I still have the occasional nightmare, but I do feel better since I've got it all off my chest, so to speak. Thanks to you.'

'Can't take credit for that – you had a helluva shock when you realized I'm an impostor, but with a little more good luck you'll be fine soon.'

'And then what?' she asked, very serious.

'Good question.' But he had an answer.

He had taken her brother's identity and, as Doc Field had pointed out, the real Jubal's responsibilities went with that action: so, *he* was obligated to take care of Andy.

CHAPTER 10

WILDERNESS

The cabin was solidly built. Doc's son, Ross, had taken a great deal of care in the design and making it as permanent as possible. The log walls were all notched and tree-nailed, the gaps plastered with a mix of mud and cement that was durable and lasting.

There was no glass in the windows – that had been too expensive, though Doc claimed Ross intended to add framed glass at a later date. The front door was solid, the planks hand-sawn and planed smooth. There was a narrow rear door that led to the path going to the privy which was also built solidly and fixed to short stumps, anchored against the bitter winter winds that probed through the Tall Men and the whole of the mountain range.

Inside had been laid out in rooms: two bedrooms, a store room, and the kitchen-living area, dominated by the big stone fireplace. As he had been told, the chimney was only made of roofing iron, but it was clear by the studs left exposed by Ross that he had fully intended to continue the fireplace, raising and shaping it into a stone chimney.

'With enough grub, and plenty of wood, we could stand a winter siege here,' opined Jubal.

Andy was sweeping the floor, mostly planked, but an area in the kitchen around the fireplace was still only hammered earth. She looked up sharply.

'I hope to be back on the stage long before winter comes.'

He met her gaze and nodded slowly. 'Just thinking aloud. Young Ross had big plans, it seems. I wouldn't mind having a place like this.'

'I thought you were going back to Texas? To start your breeding programme?'

'Yeah, I'm committed to that and I want to do it. But I might end up this way working with Bryce Pendleton and while the mountains aren't ideal for running cows, there're well-grassed flats down between the hills that could be used. Might make Doc an offer for this place.'

'You're ambitious.'

He laughed shortly. 'More like dreamin'. I've never been able to put down roots for long. But I am keen to get this breeding thing underway. You going to make the stage your career?'

She smiled and it seemed to iron out the worry lines that had appeared around her mouth as she slowly came to terms with the long-ago loss of her family.

'It *is* my career.'

'Of course it is – sorry.'

'Oh, I know it's small time and there's not much money to be made, but I like it.'

'More than half the battle, liking what you do.'

She started sweeping again and he went outside to cut more wood for the fire. He had stripped to the waist and was sheened with sweat, muscles bulging from swinging the double-bitted axe when she came out of the cabin with two mugs of coffee.

Gratefully he thunked the axe into the log and they sat down on it. He sipped the coffee and tried to hide the grimace. She looked concerned.

'I'm not very good at making coffee – or cooking in general – as you've probably noticed.'

'It's too hot, that's all,' he lied but she smiled and shook her head.

'You're a far better cook than I am.'

'Had more practice likely, a matter of self-preservation in the army. Only someone with a death wish ate what the so-called cooks turned out on those field kitchens.' He sipped again, swallowed without grimacing – just. 'I'm no expert, but I could teach you a little basic stuff – if you wanted.'

'Yes!' she said, as if that was a good idea she wished she had thought of. 'It's a talent that'll always come in handy, and – while you're in a teaching mood – could you teach me how to shoot?'

He looked at her over the rim of the mug. 'You want to learn that?'

'It's another talent that might some day come in handy.'

'Why d'you think so? Your audiences can't be that bad.'

She laughed, and he noticed how it had a more relaxed sound than when they had first arrived – when she used to force a little gaiety. It was more natural now.

He was glad it was.

'I – Pa taught all the kids how to shoot very early. I wasn't old enough but I remember I was eager to learn. Just to be like the others, I suppose, but I like guns – which I guess is unusual in a woman.'

'Yeah, it is, but you'll find most women on the frontier, living outside the towns, leastways, have been taught how to shoot by their men. If the men have any sense, that is.'

'Well, I don't intend to live in the wilderness, but I'd still like you to teach me.'

'You seemed to handle that derringer confidently enough.'

She blushed a little. 'That – well, I couldn't miss at that range, could I? And it's the simplest firearm to use – just cock the hammer and the trigger pops out, then you pull.'

'OK, six-guns and rifles are a little more compli-cated. Let's get the cabin set up for a bit more comfort and we'll have a few lessons.'

'What about the cooking?' she asked with a gleam in her eye, trying not to smile.

He tugged at one ear. 'I guess I might keep on doin' the meals for a while – don't want to confuse you with learning too many things at once.'

She laughed again. 'Too bad I left that derringer in the bottom of my bag! But I think I already know the difference between a trigger and a skillet!'

'Hey, that's a good start.'

She looked at him with mock anger. 'You're just lucky I'm not holding a skillet right now!'

'Yes, ma'am – I'll just finish my coffee and get right back to choppin' wood.'

Wichita wasn't a big man. About five feet eight inches, weight around 140 pounds. His size was made more noticeable by the twin guns he wore on a *buscadero* rig around his slim waist. He had a mocking mouth that seemed set in a half-leer, a thin nose, hooked like an Indian's and receding black hair beneath a black, high-crowned hat. His eyes were mean, or he could make them look mean when he wanted to, and mostly he worked at that full time.

The horse he rode was a big claybank, now heavily dusted and begrimed from the long trail up from Albuquerque. He sat relaxed in the saddle, but rode with gloved hands raised off his thighs, reins looped through loosely. The claybank seemed to react to small movements of his thighs, knees and heels. His boots were small and had real silver spurs attached, but without rowels.

His clothes, though trail-stained, were good quality range gear; calfskin vest over a denim shirt with dark blue edging around the collar, trousers dark brown corduroy, with a mud stain on the outside of his left knee. Beside him, Gale rode sloppily, slouched in the saddle, under his strangely mangled hat, his well-worn working clothes even more stained than Wichita's, a shirt tail half-out, boots scuffed, heels worn. His spurs had rowels, a couple of spikes broken off each.

Both men were stubbled and after leaving their mounts at the livery with the packhorses, they went to the barber's.

He was offering hot baths out back in big empty tallow kegs for twenty-five cents and both men had one each after a shave and hair trim.

Wichita didn't care for his trail-dirty clothes although he put them on, grimacing a little. Gale dressed hurriedly like it was breakfast time in the bunkhouse, didn't seem to care how the gritty clothes felt against his newly bathed body.

'I'm gonna buy a new outfit,' Wichita said, looking around. He spied the big sign *Liddell's General Store* and gestured towards it.

'These'll do me for a spell yet before I have to throw 'em away,' Gale said. 'I'm goin' for a drink.'

'See you there a little later,' Wichita said and crossed the street towards the store.

Gale sauntered down the walk to the nearest saloon, his throat contracting at the sight of a poster advertising beer frothing over the rim of a large glass. . . .

Wichita was served by Liddell himself and the storekeeper was mighty pleased with the man's choice of quality shirt and trousers, and his preference for a plain, soft, black leather vest to the calfskin one he now wore.

'Going to cost you most of seven dollars, my friend.'

'Money well spent.' The gunfighter placed a ten dollar note on the counter and while Liddell made change and started to wrap the clothes in brown paper, Wichita said casually, 'Come up from Albuquerque – picked up a Santa Fe *Gazette* to read and help pass the time. You see that article about the stage show gal up here and the massacre in Texas?'

Liddell nodded soberly. 'She collapsed on stage, you know.'

'Yeah, so it said. Part I was interested in was this brother – Jubal Mann.' Liddell seemed suddenly wary but waited for the man to continue. 'I was in the war with a Jubal Mann, as I recall, he said he was from Texas. Wonderin' if it could be the same feller.'

'Possible, I suppose.'

'He still in town, d'you know? I'd like to look him up.' Wichita smiled, soft and friendly. 'There're a few wild nights when we had leave I'd like to remind him of.' He winked, smiled wider, shaking his head. 'He could sure sink that redeye, old Jube.'

Liddell sobered. 'Well, the Jubal Mann that was here didn't seem to drink much.'

'Aw, he'd have more sense now. He still here then?'

Liddell shook his head slowly. 'You'd have to ask Doc Field.'

Wichita's smile faded. 'He's hurt?'

'No, no, but I hear Doc sent him and his sister somewhere she could rest and get over this thing that made her pass out on stage. . . .'

Wichita nodded, looking relieved, got directions for the doctor's place and walked out with his parcel under his arm. . . .

The young trainee nurse, a local girl in her teens named Elvira, opened the door to Wichita and Gale who he had picked up at the saloon on the way. She wore small wire-framed spectacles and squinted at the strangers.

'Wanta see the doc,' Wichita said, moving in and forcing her to stand back. He pressed against the door with a shoulder and her small resistance was of no avail. Gale crowded in too, smelling of booze. Elvira was frightened, by Gale and his dirty clothes, and by the other man with twin guns. She turned and hurried away calling for the doctor.

Wichita and Gale strode quickly after her and followed her into the infirmary where Doc Field was standing, with a kidney bowl that contained a bottle and some tubing. He looked past the girl to the two men.

'Thank you, Elvira. You can go home now but be sure you come in half an hour earlier tonight for your shift, all right?'

'Yes, Doctor,' she said and made a brief curtsey, hurrying through to the rear of the infirmary. There were three patients; a woman who lay on her back, snoring lightly, a man with arm and shoulder in a plaster cast, his injured arm standing upright in the cast, free of the bedclothes, like a signal. The third patient was Link Barnes.

He was propped up in bed, dozing, his face decorated with several strips of adhesive plaster and cotton wadding now instead of the cumbersome bandage. The one over his busted nose was shaped and stiffer than the others. He looked at the trio with hooded eyes, only half awake.

'How can I help you gents?' Doc asked.

'Was tellin' the storekeeper I was in the army with a feller named Jubal Mann and wondered if he was the same one that that feller Stewart wrote about. Seems you sent him off somewhere with the gal. . . .'

Field was wary: he had been on the frontier long enough to pick a gunfighter when he saw one. And Wichita definitely had the mark. Gale, too, in his shapeless hat and grimy clothes looked as if he could kill a man without turning a hair.

'Oh, they've been gone for a week or more now,' the doctor hedged.

'Gone where, Doc?' pushed Wichita, still smiling pleasantly, except his eyes were mean and cold like a hunting lizard's. 'That's what we want to know.'

'Oh, I should think they'd probably be in Denver by now. They were going to catch a train at Boulder Junction and—'

'No, Doc!' Wichita broke in, raising his voice, while Gale watched the patients, especially Barnes who seemed to be wide awake now and taking an interest. 'Storekeeper said you were sendin' the woman somewhere quiet to rest up, shake all the troubles that were botherin' her.'

Field nodded vigorously. 'Yes, yes – to a colleague of mine down in Denver! Good Lord, man, she couldn't travel alone and Jubal Mann is her brother, so he went as her escort.'

Wichita frowned and stared hard at the medic. 'Don't believe you, Doc. What you say, Gale?'

'He's lyin'.'

'Look, you asked me for help and I'm trying to oblige. . . .'

'He's lyin', all right.'

Both men turned quickly as Barnes spoke, his words slurred because of his broken teeth and smashed mouth.

'He sent 'em up into the mountains, to a cabin his son built a couple years ago. I can take you to the general area but I dunno where it is exactly.'

'Damn you, Link!' snapped the doctor and Wichita pushed past him, jerking his head at Gale, who drew his gun and held it on Field.

'Who're you?' Wichita demanded from the end of Barnes's bed.

'Used to be the deputy,' Barnes said bitterly. 'Damn sheriff fired me 'cause I sold the gal's story to the *Clarion*.'

'Sheriff Gower should've run you out of town!' snapped the medic and Wichita looked at him sharply.

'Luke Gower?' When Field nodded slowly, Wichita smiled. 'Hear that, Gale? Old Luke Gower – fastest gun in the Big Sky Country they used to say.'

'Aw, hold up, Wichita! We don't need that kinda trouble.'

'What kinda trouble?' Wichita asked innocently. 'Hell, no sheriff worth his salt'd back down when he found a man with my rep in town – and not wantin' to leave.'

'The Skipper don't want that—'

The doctor suddenly made a dash for the door that Elvira had gone through. The young nurse was just opening it and they collided. She was in her street clothes now and staggered as Wichita grabbed the sawbones' collar and hurled him hard against the wall. She screamed and put her hands over her face.

'Shut up, you stupid bitch!' yelled Gale and started towards her.

Wichita put out a hand and stopped him, looking at the frightened girl. 'No – you go ahead and scream, missy. Scream your lungs out!'

Gale swore. 'You want Gower to come runnin', don't you?'

Wichita didn't answer as the girl shook her head now, cowering, her face half-covered with shaking hands. The gunfighter smiled at her, reached for the dazed doctor and slammed him back against the wall again. Field's head struck the wood hard and his legs sagged. Wichita grabbed his right hand, splayed it against the wall and drew a gun with his own left hand. He tossed the Colt up and caught it, reversed now, the butt uppermost.

It moved with the speed of a striking snake and bones crunched in the medic's fingers. He gagged and fell to his knees, clutching the broken digits across his chest, teeth gritted, as he moaned in great pain.

'As good as breakin' a gunslinger's trigger finger,' opined Wichita and kicked Field in the ribs, forcing a deep grunt from him.

Any other sounds he made were drowned by the series of piercing screams that came from Elvira's wide open mouth.

She could be heard over most of this part of town, including the law office.

CHAPTER 11

GUNFIGHT

Sheriff Luke Gower was halfway through his office door when two townsmen came running up, looking wild-eyed and worried, one pointing across to the side street where Doc Field had his infirmary.

'Judas, Sheriff! Sounds like someone's bein' raped!'

'Or killed,' suggested the second man.

'I ain't deaf,' snapped Gower, settling his gunbelt, taking time to tie the leather thong that held down the base of his cut-out holster around his thigh.

'Don't just sound like Doc pullin' teeth or cuttin' into someone, do it?'

'Idiot! He'd knock 'em out with something first!' Gower was moving fast towards the side street where the screams could still be heard, though maybe there was a slightly longer gap between them now, like the screamer was running out of breath.

'Where the hell you think you're goin'?' Gower snapped as the two townsmen trailed him, and several other men came running, all turning into the street.

'See what's happenin'!' gasped an out-of-condition barfly.

'Stay back! This is official law business!'

'We elected you, Luke!'

'Yeah, we got a right to know what's goin' on.'

Gower said no more, feeling the effort of half-running, forcing himself to slow down. Then as they came into sight of the infirmary, he stopped in his tracks, causing a brief chaos as other men collided and all dodged around him.

Standing at the gate of Doctor Field's house was Wichita – just standing there with his arms hanging loosely at his sides, the insides of his wrists brushing his gun butts.

'By hell, you're an old man now, Gower!' he called.

The sheriff squinted, straining to make out the gunfighter's identity.

'Wichita Pell? Thought someone had collected the bounty on you long since, you backshootin' son of a bitch.'

Wichita smiled at the insult. 'That's it, Gower! That's it! Get nice an' riled, 'cause this is as far as you go – an' you don't even get the chance to enjoy any retirement. Tsk, tsk, tsk! Ain't it sad?'

'Don't be stupid. First, you gotta nail me, then you're not just a killer, you're a mad dog who shot a lawman. You'll be hunted down in a month. . . .'

'Dream on, old man. You won't be the first badge-toter I've killed.' He moved his feet a shade and grinned as Gower tensed and moved his right hand an inch closer to his gun butt. 'No – not just yet. I gotta remind you *why*?'

'You don't. Your damn brother was even cockier and stupider than you – and he was way slower than me.'

Wichita's face was heavy now, mean eyes slitted. 'That's the difference between Nat an' me – I'm way faster. *See*!'

The crowd that had gathered scattered, as, without further warning, Wichita's twin guns came up blazing.

Gower put in a good effort, a *damn* good effort, but he was just that hair slower and Wichita's bullets hammered into him and thrust him back violently just before he got off his own shot. It was the only one he would make – *could* make, because Wichita's lead had exploded his heart and his lean body twisted like a corkscrew as it tumbled towards the ground.

The crowd were staring as Wichita walked up, stood over the dead sheriff and pumped two more bullets into him, his body jerking.

The gunman raked his bleak gaze around the shocked audience. 'My brother reared me after a damn posse killed my old man.' He kicked Gower, moving the body a couple of inches. 'This son of a bitch was leadin' it!'

He knew there was no danger of anyone in the crowd trying to avenge the sheriff. He arrogantly took time to reload his guns, then walked back towards Doc Field's house.

'Move that garbage off the street,' he tossed over his shoulder as he went inside and almost fell over Elvira where she lay on the floor. 'The hell happened to her?'

Gale grinned. 'Fainted dead away.'

Then Wichita saw the doctor spread out on his face, a trickle of blood showing through his matted hair.

'Christ, you didn't kill him!'

Gale shook his head. 'Had a lotta guts for an old sawbones. Was tryin' for that cupboard with the door open, nursin' the hand you busted.'

Wichita could see the butt of a Smith & Wesson pistol on the shelf, grunted, and looked back to Barnes's bed.

'You nail Gower?' Link asked and when Wichita said nothing he added, 'Hell, wish you'd waited till I got there! He's been ridin' me hard lately.'

'No more. Now, how about this damn cabin where I'll find Mann and the gal?'

Barnes flicked his gaze from Wichita to Gale, ran the tip of his tongue lightly across his mangled lips.

'Er – there's a bounty on Jubal, ain't there. . . ? Five thousand I heard.'

'Up to six now,' Gale said flatly.

Wichita waited: he knew what was coming.

'That's OK.' Barnes was breathing more quickly and

134

deeply now. 'We – we split even-Steven, three ways. . . . ? Makes two thousand apiece. Pretty good, huh?'

Gale snorted. 'Who's cuttin' you in for a share?'

Barnes managed a part grin, before beads of blood squeezed out of his puffed lip and made him wince.

'I know the way—'

' "General area", you said,' Gale reminded him.

'It's three-parts done once we get on to the right mountain.'

'An' you reckon that entitles you to a third share of the bounty?'

'Well, yeah. I mean, I'm the only one knows that much now: Doc won't be no good. He couldn't make the ride into that kinda country an' he'll be out for a long time.'

Gale looked at Wichita who was just staring at Barnes, though sure not in friendly manner.

'You see what happened to Doc?' Gale asked Barnes. 'He'll be lucky if he can ever operate again. We finished him in the sawbones business except for cuts an' bruises, or mebbe helpin' some woman whelp. What could we do to you? A mean bastard of a deputy, already smashed up by this Jubal?' He turned to Wichita. 'What you reckon? Bullet through both feet – or hands?'

'Hey, Judas, wait up!'

Gale put a hand behind his ear. 'I hear you say you ain't gonna push for a third of the bounty. . . ?'

Barnes swallowed. 'Well – I-I figure I could be due somethin'. . . .'

' 'Course you are, Deputy,' spoke up Wichita. 'Gale, he's gotta get somethin' for his trouble – be fair now.'

Gale caught a passing look on Wichita's face that he'd seen before. . . . *Sure! Barnes would be paid off for his trouble, right enough!* But mebbe not in cash. . . .

'Yeah, guess you're right. OK, Barnes. Get yourself ready. You take us to the cabin and we'll see you right.'

Link Barnes felt a hollowness in his belly, but greed overcame it and he sat on the edge of the bed, stooping down with a grunt to pick up his boots.

'The crowd won't give you no trouble?' he asked. 'I mean, Gower was popular. . . .'

'So? Let 'em give him a big funeral then. Hurry it up, or there could be two funerals.'

Barnes smiled thinly, ignoring the pain it cost him now.

'Nah – that's one thing I ain't worried about. Not till we find the cabin, leastways.'

Wichita made a 'what-do-you-think-of-that' gesture with his mouth as he slanted his head slightly. 'Hey, man's got more guts than I give him credit for.'

'You might be surprised,' Barnes said and immediately wished he hadn't, the way the two killers looked at him.

He hurriedly pulled on his boots. His face hurt from the stooping and he couldn't breathe properly.

Hell, if these two only knew it, he'd gladly do it for nothing, just so he could either kill Jubal – or watch while they did it.

But he wasn't about to let them know that.

Jubal had reached the sad conclusion that Andy was never going to make a great cook. Maybe not even a modest one.

She just didn't have the touch, couldn't seem to get a sense of how hot the fire had to be or how hot it was under the cast-iron pot or skillet.

He liked crunchy bacon but. . . !

'Not very good is it?' she asked as they both crunched away at the charred offerings on the plate with the dried-out corn fritters and the last of the hen eggs with the busted yolks.

'Takes a while to figure out how hot to make the skillet or hot plate,' he said non-committally. 'We've got that jackrabbit I shot. He's big enough to make a stew for us with the last of the vegetables Liddell gave us.'

She wiped her mouth on the rag she was using as a table napkin, washed down the charred bacon with a sip of coffee, grimaced.

'I think, rather than risk wasting the rabbit, now that you've skinned and gutted it, we should leave it for now – and you can show me how to use a gun.'

He thought it was a good idea, too, but didn't want to seem too enthusiastic – he was trying to figure out how he could take over making the stew without hurting her feelings.

'Well, time's gettin' on – hour or two to sundown. We could start the stew and leave it simmering – I can dig a hole and line it with coals and then cover the lid of the pot with a layer of dirt and hot ash. It'll hold in the heat and cook away – be ready by the time we get back.'

She was showing genuine interest in that. 'Sounds like a – a pioneer idea.'

'The old hunters often did that. Makes a fine meal – and that appetizing smell when you get back to camp. . . .'

She laughed. 'All right! You do it – you show me how. That way at least we'll have had one good meal this day!'

He smiled crookedly. 'That obvious, was I?'

'You were – I don't mind, Jubal. I'm not going to be offended. You're not the first person who's tried to teach me to cook. I just don't seem to have any knack in that direction.' She sobered and sighed. 'Lord knows what I'll do if ever I get married.'

'When you're a famous actress, you'll be able to afford to eat out – or pay your own cook.'

'Well, that's one possible solution – if ever I become a famous actress.'

'You're doing OK so far – I didn't see very much of that *Midsummer Dream* or whatever it was called, but you seemed to do well, enjoyed your work.'

'Yes, I do enjoy it.'

'All right, let's go see how you shoot. Wear a jacket and take a towel or petticoat you can roll up and stuff into the top of the jacket sleeve.'

'What for?'

He pointed to the Winchester. 'It'll kick, not a lot to anyone who's used to it, but for someone just learning, the recoil can leave bruises.'

When she was ready, he took up the rifle and some boxes of ammunition and they left the crumbled black bacon pieces on their plates with the shrivelled eggs and went out into the afternoon.

He had already picked out a clearing where he could set up targets. He had brought along some empty bottles from the trash pit behind the cabin, half-filled a few with creek water: they'd look mighty spectacular when the bullet shattered the glass and the water erupted with the sunlight behind it. Gave the learner-shooter a thrill and eagerness to do it again – as often as possible.

But first he showed her how to hold the Winchester.

'For some reason most women never seem comfortable the way they hold a rifle – they tend to lean back to counter the weight, makes 'em unsteady on their feet, or gives 'em a creak in the spine if they're lying prone. You have to snug the curve of the butt plate firmly into your shoulder. It'll fit if you do – and don't stretch your arm to hold the fore-end. You just don't have balance and the rifle will kick like a mule, make you feel like you've busted your shoulder and shoot all over the place. We'll practice that for twenty minutes or so before we get you to shoot.'

She looked up at the sky through the branches of the overhead trees as they swayed in a light breeze.

'It'll be getting dark soon, won't it?'

'Yeah, night tends to come quickly in the mountains, lots of shadows and so on, but you'll get a couple of shots in. Make you eager to get back to it tomorrow. . . .' *I hope*!

She looked at him soberly. 'You're enjoying this, aren't you? Being the teacher.'

'Andy, I'm enjoying being able to show you something useful. You travel a lot on the frontier, you're a fine-looking woman and – well, there're a lot more men than women up here and sometimes they forget who belongs to who.'

She smiled slowly. 'I'm not sure about that "belongs" part, but I see what you mean. And I'm grateful, Jubal. You – you're acting just like an amiable big brother.'

'Like as if I was the real Jubal?' She nodded, and he added, 'I told you I was prepared to take on what would've been Jubal's responsibilities if he'd still been alive. It's no chore, Andy. It's a pleasure.'

Her smile widened. 'I may've been too young to remember my brother, but I – I'm glad I have *this* Jubal to help me.'

Darkness caught the hunters just as they entered the section of the mountains known as the Tall Men.

The ride had taken a good deal out of Link Barnes, and he had called for frequent rests until Wichita impatient, had laid it on the line.

'You're the one who's ailin', Barnes. This Jubal is the *hombre* who beat the crap outta you. Figured you'd be more eager to run him down.'

'I am! Judas, I want to nail that sonuver so bad I haven't been able to sleep!'

Wichita leaned from the saddle, resting a hand on Barnes's thigh as their horses moved a little. Wichita's gaze locked on to Barnes's battered face.

'Then quit all this stop-startin'! Get the hell along the trail and let's find the son of a bitch and get the chore done! Savvy? No – more – rests!'

Barnes savvied but he didn't feel any better. He was weaker than he had figured and knew he really needed another day, or a couple of days' bed rest. But he made no protest – not the way these two killers looked at him. . . .

The rock columns of the Tall Men towered above their camp place and once the sun was behind them, they built up the fire and reached for their jackets.

'Don't make that fire too damn big,' warned Gale. 'We dunno where this cabin is and if they see the glow. . . .'

It was good advice, but they shivered through the night and Wichita said the hell with it, and threw more wood on the breakfast fire. It flared up and Gale glared at him.

'Dammit! I thought I warned you about the fire!'

'So? They'll likely smell the smoke anyway.'

Barnes agreed but wished he had kept quiet when he saw Gale's deadly stare. *They didn't really care what he thought. He was only tolerated because he was useful.*

'Well, let's get the eatin' done and then move on. That'll warm us up if nothin' else.'

They were packing the breakfast things away when the gunfire came rolling down the timbered slopes – more or less evenly-spaced shots.

'Rifle,' allowed Barnes unnecessarily.

'Just one,' Gale said. 'Mebbe huntin' grub.'

'Forget the "mebbes" and get a direction,' growled Wichita, checking his Colts. 'With a little luck, this chore might be over by noon.' He half-smiled. 'Then we'll all be rich, eh, Barnes?

The ex-deputy nodded slowly: there was something taunting in Wichita's words.

He poured himself a cup of coffee with a hand that shook a little. He didn't want anything to eat.

He'd suddenly lost his appetite.

CHAPTER 12

THE TALL MEN

The bottle was dirty and three-parts full of murky creek water, but when it exploded, on Andy's fifth shot, it suddenly turned into a flowering of sparkling diamonds and water patterns that reminded her of a ballet's beauty.

To Jubal, it was just a good shot – maybe a *lucky* shot – but it looked spectactular and he saw the almost childish pleasure on her face, lighting her eyes, bringing a smile and even a laugh as she rolled on to her side.

'I hit it! I hit the target!'

'Yeah – good shootin',' he told her, although it was only thirty feet away and it wasn't often you got that close to a living, hostile target. Still, add the size of a human body and do a little fancy calculation, and he was willing to allow that it was likely equivalent to seventy or eighty feet against a live target – which was good shooting.

'You're getting the hang of it pretty fast.'

She was rubbing her right shoulder, although she had packed a rolled hand towel under her jacket.

'Some of me's getting used to it.'

'Hold it more firmly. *Pull* the rifle in against your shoulder – leave just a quarter-inch gap and you're gonna have a bruise and a sore spot to remind you you didn't do it properly.'

'Huh! Nice of you to be so sympathetic.'

He sighed. 'I think that's about the tenth time I've told you.'

She pursed her lips then smiled and nodded. 'I know! I'm sorry – it's my own fault.'

'You want to wait a spell before you try again.'

'No! Not on your life. There're still two more bottles standing and – how many more bullets in the gun?'

'*Cartridges* in the *rifle*,' he corrected her automatically. 'There're six left. Now take your time. You're excited and—'

The rifle crashed and when the smoke cleared the two bottles were still standing on the log. She frowned at him and he shrugged.

'Take – your – time. Breathe deep but slow, and just squeeze the trigger. That time you jerked and the barrel jumped three or four inches high. Try again.'

Mouth set determinedly, she took so long to shoot he wondered if there had been a misfire he hadn't heard. Then the Winchester gave its characteristic whipcrack and he heard her say, feelingly, '*Ouch!*'

and he knew her shoulder had taken a beating again.

And the two bottles were still standing.

He went to the small camp-fire where he had left a coffee pot warming, poured two mugs and took them across.

She refused the cup he offered. 'I'm going to get those two damn bottles if it takes me all day!'

'As well it might if you don't calm down. You did it once and I savvy how your blood's singing and you're eager to do it again and again. But you've got to learn to relax in between shots.'

'How can you?'

'Well, you need to. It's easy when you're only potting at targets – not so easy when someone's shooting back at you.'

She looked thoughtful and automatically accepted the coffee this time when he proferred it. She drank almost half before she realized it, looked startled, then smiled sheepishly. 'Control – that's what you're teaching me, isn't it?'

'I figure you know a deal about control, acting on stage. Just transfer some of it to your shooting.'

'Now I understand – I'm sorry for being such a fool at it.'

They drank their coffee and she asked him for the makings, and he watched as she expertly built a cigarette. She took a match from his shirt pocket, scraped it on a log and lit up, smiling as she exhaled.

'Haven't you heard about us theatre people. . . ? Smoking, drinking, loose with our morals. . . ?' He frowned and she laughed. 'I enjoy a smoke, cheroots occasionally, but I don't mind rolling my own – steadies my nerves before a performance. I hardly ever take a drink, and as for the morals. . . .'

He held up a hand. 'That's your business. Finish the cigarette, then get back to your target practice.'

'Have I shocked you?'

'I dunno. Not used to talkin' about such things with ladies, is all. Make the subject guns, or cows. . . .'

She laughed. 'You're poking fun at me! All right – I'll have two more drags and then it's back to the bottles.'

She hit the remaining two bottles with the next three shots. The explosions weren't quite as spectacular as the first because the sun had risen higher and the rays were at a different angle.

'That's damn good, and I'm not just saying it so as to encourage you. We'll move back to fifty feet this time.'

'Isn't that a little far?'

Soberly, he told her, 'It's about as close as you ever want to get to someone who's shooting back at you. 'Fact, you'll wish it was a hundred, or a hundred-fifty feet.'

The thought sobered her and they set up with empty bottles this time.

'My God! They look so small!' she exclaimed as he settled her in a prone position behind a deadfall.

'About twice as big as a man's heart would be at that distance.'

She grimaced. 'Don't say things like that!'

'You wanted to know how to use a gun. You didn't

146

figure you'd only be shooting at targets, did you?'

Her teeth tugged at her bottom lip and she looked thoughtful, then gave a single shake of her head.

'No, of course not. . . .'

But he knew she hadn't thought about exchanging bullets with someone trying to kill her. 'Don't worry about it – it may never happen. But – if it does. . . .'

'You – you'd better show me how to use a six-shooter, too.'

He smiled. 'Now you're getting the idea. Learn it all and if you never have to use it – be thankful.'

'*And* be thankful if I *do*!'

'That's it.'

In the end he had to make her stop. 'You're gonna have a mighty sore shoulder. You're holding the rifle better, just about right, but those early mistakes have – literally – left their mark, I'll bet.'

She moved her right arm slowly, rubbing at the shoulder. 'I'm afraid you're right. What about the six-gun?'

He smiled at her eagerness. 'I'll just give you a rundown on what you do and how to reload. Leave the shooting of it till later – this afternoon, maybe, and—'

He stopped speaking and she started to ask a question, but he lifted a hand quickly and she fell silent, frowning, heart skipping a beat as she saw the expression on his face.

'What?' she asked in a stage whisper.

'I heard a horse. No, not one of ours, it was down-slope.' He was already reloading the Winchester, thrust up. 'In the cabin – *quickly*!'

They ran to the rear door and he pushed her inside. 'Here – you take the rifle. You're used to its feel now – I'll grab the spare carbine.'

She held the rifle across her body as he had shown her but simply stood there while he took out the carbine from his bedroll, checked the magazine.

'Get to a window!' he snapped and saw her start to bristle at his bossy tone. 'You want to stay alive?' he added.

She nodded, paled, and ran to one of the side windows near the front, pushing the shutter on to its first notch. By kneeling she could see underneath and she said in a shaky voice,

'There're two riders coming!'

Jubal was crouched by the big window near the front door. 'Two we can see.'

'Wh-what?'

'Could be more. One's Link Barnes. He's got enough plaster on his face to make it stand out – a good target.'

She whipped her head around, very pale now. 'No! You think they mean trouble.'

'Uh-huh.'

They had stopped now just within the line of trees. Jubal could make out the other man, a stranger wearing a battered hat. Both had rifles across their thighs and Barnes called out.

'Hello the cabin! This is Deputy Barnes, from

Cheyenne. Like to ask you some questions about a fugitive I'm trackin' in these hills. I can see someone crouchin' by a window. Gimme an answer.'

The girl jumped, even gave a small squeal, as Jubal's carbine cracked twice and bark jumped from a tree over Barnes's head. The ex-deputy wheeled instantly and drove his mount deeper into the trees. Gale started his mottled grey moving, too, but he took time to throw his rifle up and rake the front door with three shots before going out of sight among the trees.

'My God! Who are they?'

'You know Barnes – he was the one sold your story to the newspapers. I'm the one beat him up and Gower fired him. The other one is a hired gun, I'd say, the way he got those shots off.'

'But – what do they want?'

'Keep down!' he snapped as both rifles raked the cabin now. 'Just wastin' ammo, which means they want us layin' low, so we can't see what's going on.'

'What d' you mean. . . ?'

He was already moving towards the narrow rear door when it was kicked open and he glimpsed a man with two guns crouched there. He dived for the floor, rolling, bringing the carbine over in front of him as Wichita's guns hammered, bullets kicking dirt from the puncheon floor section.

Jubal's carbine triggered and he thought he heard the girl scream, noticed out of the corner of his left eye that she was lying prone on the floor. *Good thinking, or. . . ?*

149

Firing wild, his lead splintered the door-frame, one ricocheting from the wood range alongside it. It threw Wichita, and he jumped back, jumped out of line with the door. But, as Jubal leapt up, levering in a fresh load, he stepped out again swiftly, catching Mann off-guard.

Wichita's right hand gun boomed and Andy screamed as Jubal crashed to the floor, blood showing high on his left leg. He rolled in against the base log of the wall as Wichita stepped inside, both smoking guns covering Jubal and the girl, a crooked smile on his face.

'Don't be in a hurry to die, missy. Just let that rifle stay down on the floor an' you sit up against the logs.'

'Wichita!' Gale bawled from outside. 'You still breathin'?'

'Enough to cuss you for a damn fool! Get on in here an' bring that stupid deputy.'

Jubal was holding his bleeding thigh, his carbine lying two feet away from his free hand. He grimaced in pain and then the girl had crawled over to him, ignoring Wichita's instructions.

'Is – is it bad?' she asked. She looked very pale still and there was fear in her eyes, but she was game enough, Jubal thought.

'Not bad, bleedin' a fair bit. Do like he says, Andy. Don't make him mad.' He lifted his gaze to Wichita's mean face. 'I mean angry mad – he's already loco mad.'

Wichita stepped forward and ground a bootheel into Jubal's wound, forcing gritted gasps of pain from the man. Andy looked horrified, then grabbed Wichita's leg and pushed it roughly away.

'You damn sadist!' she choked.

For a moment, through the red pulsing haze of pain, Jubal thought Wichita was going to shoot her, but he stopped himself in time and smiled crookedly.

'Know somethin', missy? You ain't gonna get the quick bullet I had with your name on it. Uh-uh, you got the kinda fire I like in a woman. The Skipper never said you'd put up a fight, but you go right ahead. I'm real eager to tangle with you now!'

Barnes and Gale came, guns drawn. Wichita was standing over Jubal, left gun holstered, the other still smoking slightly as he held it casually on the wounded man.

'I-I need to bind that wound,' Andy said shakily and Wichita snapped his head around, started to lift the gun, but nodded slowly.

'Sure you do, sweetie. You do what you want. It ain't gonna make his dyin' any quicker or easier.'

She took Jubal's bandanna off and her own silk neckerchief, using the latter wadded up to cover the wound. He bent his leg a little, gritting his teeth at the painful effort, and she passed the bandanna underneath and tied it over the silk. It would put pressure on the wound and at least slow the bleeding.

Gale and Barnes watched.

'Why don't we just shoot 'em and get it over with?' the ex-deputy asked.

'Fun time, that's why.' Wichita said it casually but

there was a look on his face that brooked no argument. 'What's the big hurry? We got 'em, we can do what we like with 'em. Skipper didn't say how to kill 'em, just get it done.'

Barnes didn't look too sure but Gale smiled, showing his stained teeth. 'Easiest three grand I ever made.'

Barnes stiffened. 'You mean two don't you?'

Gale looked from Barnes to Wichita and back again. 'Yeah, sure. Just talkin' – generally, you know.'

Jubal watched Barnes's battered face, could see the man was mighty wary now: he guessed, correctly, that there was some – uneasiness – about the splitting of the bounty. . . .

'Don't expect a square deal from these sons of bitches, Barnes. You'll get what you deserve – an' wouldn't suprise me if it turns out to be nothin' but a big zero.'

He stopped abruptly as Wichita kicked him in the side. Andy reached across, protecting him with her slim body. Wichita laughed.

'By hell, missy, you are gettin' me all excited!'

'Ah, come on, you fellers!' Barnes said, sounding pained. 'Let's get it done and then telegraph to this Skipper so's we can get the bounty. I wanna clear this goddamn country quick as I can.'

'Aw, you'll be OK, Barnes,' Wichita said without looking at him. 'Me and Gale'll see you right.'

'Sure thing,' Gale said, but Jubal could see Barnes wasn't reassured.

'Well, let's get on with it, huh?'

'Who *is* this "Skipper" or "Captain" as he some-times calls himself?' Jubal said, biting back the pain in his thigh, trying to stall.

'Don't you know?' Wichita flicked his gaze to Andy and she shook her head slowly.

'Why don't you tell her, Gale? You were in on the original massacre. . . .'

Gale swore softly. 'Thanks a lot, Wichita!'

'Hell, what you worried about? These two won't be able to tell anyone.'

Gale swept his gaze towards Barnes who happened to be looking at Jubal's leg, seeing the blood soaking through the bandanna and the corduroy trousers.

'Don't worry about it,' Wichita said again.

'Why did this "Captain" kill all my family?' Andy asked, hands clenched in front of her now. 'Why did he bother to tell my mother about my father first. . . ?'

Gale shrugged. 'Funny kinda feller, Cap'n Stone. He wanted your Ma to feel real bad hurt, you kids too, before he set the Injuns on you.'

'But *why*, damn you! Why did he give her – us – that extra hurt when he knew we were going to be attacked anyway?'

'Ah, you gotta know the Cap'n, missy. He's mighty poorly right now but he had – has – a full-'n'-plenty way of hatin'. An' he hated Mel Mann. For why? Because your old man was a drunk.' He paused for Andy's reaction but she kept her face blank. 'He was soft as milk pudden. Hated the way he left you an' your kin to battle on, even though he was sendin' what money he got as wagonmaster back to your old lady. Soft as unchurned butter! It played on Mel's mind. There were boys on that wagon train who brewed their own booze, would eat through gunmetal. Old Mel, feelin' black-dog down, took on a load, weepin' and moanin' about how he was a lousy provider an' took a wrong turnin', led the wagon train right smack into the middle of Ute country. Man, them Injuns had a mighty big hate on for white folk at that time. . . .'

He paused and shrugged. 'They wiped out that wagon train, killed every livin' thing, hoss teams, mules, dogs, chickens – nothin' escaped 'em.' He looked at his audience. 'Sure not Cap'n Stone's family.'

'Dear God!' Andy exclaimed, a hand going to her mouth .

'An' I mean *all* his family; his mother and grandmother, wife, brother, all his kids, and there were seven. Cap, as the scout, see, was away at the time, lookin' ahead for water and the best graze for the animals. He heard the shootin' and yellin' an' screamin', saw the smoke from the burnin' wagons – when he got back. . . .' Gale shrugged. 'Too late.'

No one said anything.

'He threw the biggest drunk I ever did see. Took four of us to get him into bed each night. Then one mornin' he woke and for some reason din' have a hangover, hell knows why, but he said to us, he knew just what had to be done. He had to even the score, wipe out Mel's famly as it was all Mel's fault. Wipe 'em out totally, see that not a single drop of Mann blood remained on this earth. Only then would he know some peace.'

'Crazy with grief,' opined Jubal.

Gale nodded. 'You got it right. He was plumb crazy. He tracked down Mel's family and—' He looked at Andy who was trembling, face white as marble. 'Well, we had word that Jubal there had been killed in the war so Cap was satisfied with that. He never knew *you'd* got away, either, missy. But your scalp wasn't along with the others.' Andy sucked in a sharp breath, eyes glistening. 'Got one helluva shock when we seen in that newspaper story how you hadn't been buried alive after all. He knew by then Jubal was still alive and put out the bounty. You never showed up for a long spell and then that article again led us right to you.' Gale sighed, 'Old Cap is mighty poorly, but I reckon he'll hold on long enough to hear you're all dead before he cashes in his chips.'

'The world won't miss a crazy son of a bitch like him,' allowed Jubal, and Gale's eyes flared.

'You keep your mouth offa the captain, you bastard! You ain't good enough to wipe his nose!'

He stepped in, swinging a boot at Jubal's side, but the girl wrapped both arms about his leg and pulled him off balance.

'*Watch it!*' yelled Wichita warningly, swinging up his gun, but Andy's weight had dragged Gale down and he sprawled across Jubal, who grunted aloud in pain.

Wichita was jumping around so as to get a clear

shot but Barnes got in his way and they tangled.

A red haze of pain surged behind his eyes as Gale flung the girl off. Jubal snatched at Gale's gun, got it in his hand and reversed it swiftly. Gale closed and the gun muzzle was right against his chest when Jubal looked into his wild eyes and dropped the hammer.

Gale was hurled to one side and Wichita thrust Barnes off him and swung up his gun as Jubal triggered again, twice, swung the smoking barrel on to Barnes, and as the ex-deputy lifted his own Colt shot him in the chest.

Wichita was down and on his side, bringing his gun around despite the two bullets Jubal had fired into him.

'No!' cried Andy and snatched up Barnes's gun in both hands, somehow got it set in the right position and cocked the hammer, shooting instantly.

Wichita, a gunfighter who had killed fourteen men in face-off shootouts, had faced down armed marshals and outlaws alike, died by the hand of a young girl who hadn't even fired a real gun until that very morning. . . .

If he knew it in that instant before the bullet killed him, he must have gone to Hell raging.

Andy dropped the smoking gun, looking horrified at what she had done. Jubal, suffering a lot of pain now, looked up at her from the floor and forced himself to smile.

'Thanks – An-dray-uh. . . .'

She sat down heavily and didn't answer, stared at

the dead men, then looked away out the open front door at the Tall Men towering above the cabin, emblazoned now by the sun.

She looked at Jubal, a faint smile touching her lips.

'Andy is good enough,' she said.

He nodded, smiling despite the pain. 'She sure is.'

'That gal's got real guts,' Bryce Pendleton said as he stood at the end of the bed in Doc Field's infirmary, looking down at Jubal Mann.

'That she has,' allowed Jubal, staring past the rancher to where Doc Field was working on some medicines, using his good hand, the young nurse Elvira helping and checking that he had the right doseage. 'Doc's got guts, too. That hand'll never be quite as good as it was, but he ain't givin' up.'

'Why should he? This town needs a good doctor and he's about the best you'll find out here. Besides, they're already taking up a collection to send him to some bone specialist in Denver who might be able to get more movement in the hand.'

Pendleton took a yellow oblong of paper out of his pocket and held it out towards a curious Jubal.

'On the advice of our lawyer, Mr Guy Breen, I sent a wire to the sheriff of Landis County.' Jubal frowned and the rancher said, 'You know – where this Captain Stone lived? Just alerting him that Stone was involved in these assassination attempts on you and Andy. This is his reply.'

The wire said simply:

157

Too late. We buried the Captain yesterday.
Dodds, Sheriff, Landis County.

'I'm glad of that. A real son of a bitch, but twisted, I guess.' He crumpled the form and looked up. 'Bryce, I'm glad our deal's still going ahead.'

'Of course. You'll be on your feet and able to travel in a few weeks. Winter might be here by the time you get back but spring follows, and that's the time a Red Angus bull's thoughts turn to the nearest cows. Well, any time of the year, I guess, but we'll just make sure that the nearest are your longhorns. Programme'll be running by summer.'

Jubal smiled but Pendleton could see his mind wasn't entirely on the breeding programme.

'An-dray-uh is going back to the stage. Same company, but her adventures will ensure them great publicity and the manager sees a fine career for her. . . .' His voice trailed off. 'Oh! – is, er, that what you wanted to hear, Jubal. . . ?'

'What. . . ? Oh, yeah, of course.'

'But you would like her to come visit – even though she's in rehearsals for the re-opening of their *Saucy Shakespeare* show?'

'I wouldn't expect her to cut rehearsals,' Jubal said a mite shortly, sounding disappointed. 'Still. . . .'

'Quite right. I have to see Truscott again. I'll look in sometime this evening.'

'Yeah, fine.'

His leg was sore and Doc said he wouldn't be walking on it, even with the aid of a stick for another few days. A 'few' more days in bed would drive him nuts! He wanted to get out on the porch or somewhere he could see people moving about. The left hand end of Doc's porch looked up the street towards the Rialto theatre and he knew Doc had a set of field glasses. If he could borrow them – he might see Andy. . . .

He found the next day, when Doc said he could spend some time sitting up in bed, that he could just see the entrance to the Rialto through the window across from him.

'Doc, can I borrow your field glasses?' At the medic's puzzled look, he added. 'Give me somethin' to look at. I'm goin' kinda cabin-crazy here starin' at these walls.'

'Oh, yes, Elvira can bring them to you. Just don't move that leg around too much.'

In the afternoon, eyes watering from staring so hard and long through the magnifying lenses, he saw Andy.

He gave a little jump that hurt his wound and he bit back a curse, adjusted focus slightly.

She was wearing that green and ivory outfit she had had on when she first appeared at his hotel room door. With the bright sun on her red hair and her face, only seen dimly because of the half-veil she was wearing, she made a damn fine picture.

He felt disappointment as she started up the board-walk, away from Doc's street, one of the male actors from the show beside her, holding her elbow.

He sat there nursing the glasses, mouth tight.

Well, he knew she was mighty busy, but had hoped she might have found time to pay him a visit.

Oh, well, when I can hobble around again, I'll likely go see the show.

He was about to put the glasses under the pillow, but decided to take one more look. He tensed as he saw her, freeing her arm from the man: she seemed angry, or at least annoyed. The man blinked and stood, watching her with his mouth open as she turned and crossed the street, heading directly towards Doctor Field's house.

He still held the glasses, began to lift them towards his eyes, then stuffed them under the pillows.

Hell, what did he need the glasses for? He heard her knock on the door, then Elvira's voice, and Andy asking for him and her footsteps tap-tapping towards the infirmary section.

He fixed his gaze on the door, holding his breath as he waited for it to open and admit her. *He couldn't remember his heart ever pounding so damn hard!*

When she entered, she was smiling warmly, this beautiful young woman hurrying towards his bed, almost running.

Truly, the last Mann.